ALEX LA GUMA was born in 1925, son of one of the le␣␣␣r
figures in the non-white liberation movement. As a youn␣
man he joined the Communist Party, and was a member ␣
Cape Town district committee until 1950, when it was banned.
In 1956 he helped to organize the South African
representatives who drew up the Freedom Charter, and
consequently was among the 156 accused at the Treason Trials
of the same year. In 1960 he began writing for *New Age*, a
progressive newspaper, and in 1962 was put under house
arrest. Before his five-year sentence could elapse, a No Trial
Act was passed and he and his wife were put into solitary
confinement. On their release from prison they returned to
house arrest, eventually fleeing to Britain in 1967. They
moved to Cuba, where La Guma was the ANC representative.
He died in 1985.

Alex La Guma's first work was a collection of short stories
called *A Walk in the Night* (1962). It was followed by *And a
Threefold Cord, The Stone Country, In the Fog of the Seasons' End*,
and *Time of the Butcherbird*.

ALEX LA GUMA

IN THE FOG
OF THE
SEASONS' END

HEINEMANN

Heinemann International Literature and Textbooks
A division of Heinemann Educational Books Ltd
Halley Court, Jordan Hill, Oxford OX2 8EJ

Heinemann Educational Books Inc
361 Hanover Street, Portsmouth, New Hampshire, 03801, USA

Heinemann Educational Books (Nigeria) Ltd
PMB 5205, Ibadan
Heinemann Educational Boleswa
PO Box 10103, Village Post Office, Gaborone, Botswana

LONDON EDINBURGH PARIS MADRID
ATHENS BOLOGNA MELBOURNE
SYDNEY AUCKLAND SINGAPORE TOKYO

© Alex La Guma 1972
First published by Heinemann Educational Books Ltd
in the African Writers Series in 1972
Reprinted ten times
First published in this edition by
Heinemann International Literature and Textbooks
in 1992

British Library Cataloguing in Publication Data
A catalogue record for this book is available from the British Library

ISBN 0 435 90980 0

Printed and bound in Great Britain by
Cox & Wyman Ltd, Reading, Berkshire

92 93 94 10 9 8 7 6 5 4 3 2 1

In memory of Basil February
and others killed in action,
Zimbabwe, 1967.

Banquets of black entrails of the Black,
Armour of parchment of wax,
Fragile and fugitive when facing the burning stone,
Will be shattered like the spider web,
In the fog of the seasons' end.

From *Martyrs* by Conte Saidon Tidiany (Guinea)

PROLOGUE

They arrested him late one night and took him out to a Volkswagen, one of several cars which had been used in the raid. The night was still warm then in the late summer, but far out in the sky a thin mist frosted the stars like a veil flung over the spangles of a bride. Two detectives went in the car with him, one driving and the other beside him in the back, while the rest of the posse searched the house.

'We will have to book him in at the local station first,' the one beside him said. While the second detective sat beside the prisoner the driver spoke into a radio transmitter and reported the arrest to the chief of the security force for that region.

They drove through the suburban slum, past ramshackle houses, into a built-up area. The detectives did not speak to him at all on the way to the Police Station.

Some hours later, early in the morning, they came to collect him again, to take him to the Security headquarters in the city. The same detective drove the Volkswagen; he was tall and young and drove skilfully. The one in the sporting clothes was beside the prisoner again and he flexed his hands from time to time, looking at them. They drove through the waking suburbs, the haze of the ending summer's night lifting from the roofs and the gardens, the queues of early workers waiting at the bus-stops. The suburbs passed quickly and the city skimmed into sight: a serrated horizon of office blocks with rows of parking-meters like regiments of armless robots in front of them. The prisoner sat quite still and his face was set with an expression of concentration.

The detective beside him noticed this and said, 'Thinking of the story you are going to tell us?' He uttered a short bark which was meant to be a laugh. 'You are going to tell us some kind of a story,' he grinned. 'But we are not going to believe it. Do you think we are fools, you baboon?'

In front, the young one laughed heartily. 'He won't be in any mood for fairy-tales when we are through with him.'

The morning sunlight crept into the city, painting concrete and marble and metal with its first orange warmth. A trolley-bus hissed by them, heavy-laden.

'He will ask for a lawyer,' the young one laughed, watching the road ahead. 'Suddenly these things have acquired lawyers. Who ever heard of it?'

The one in the sports clothes jabbed the prisoner with an elbow. 'Too bad, *meneer*,' he said mockingly. 'No more lawyers. Those times are past. We don't give a bogger for them. We even keep the magistrates away now.'

'We'll make you shit,' the driver said viciously.

The Volkswagen turned into the street where stood the Central Police Station and the law courts: a big grey truck was unloading the previous day's crop of arrests for the magistrates. A cleaner in brown overalls swished the wide pavement with a hose and the water started to dry at once in the morning sun. They turned into a courtyard through a wide archway; the yard had been washed and smelled of disinfectant. A convict in a red shirt carried a tray of tea things through a heavy door.

The prisoner was taken along empty corridors lined with brown doors, and down some chipped stone steps. The detective in the sports clothes rapped on another door and a peephole opened, a square lid behind small bars, and then the door was unlocked. They took him down another passageway and a uniformed man with a gun and a bunch of keys opened a small room with grey walls.

'You got some time to think,' one of the detectives said. The prisoner did not look to see which one it was. 'Think it over, *kerel*, if you have brains in that skull.'

He felt a blow in his back and went head-first onto the floor. The two detectives went out and the heavy door was locked. The prisoner rolled over and sat up, his handcuffed wrists before him, and sat with his back against a grey wall. His cheekbone burned where the stone floor had grazed it. He had been anticipating a test of endurance for a long time, but now he realized that he did not really know what was going to happen to him. Behind the ugly mask of the regime was an even uglier face which he had not yet looked on. You went through the police charges in the squares, the flailing clubs, the arrogant rejection of all pleas and petitions, blood dried on the street like spilled paint where a shot body had lain, but here, behind the polished windows, the gratings and the Government paintwork, was another dimension of terror.

He did not know how long he sat there until the door crashed open again and the sportsman and the young man came in. They hauled him to his feet like a sack and rushed him roughly out into the corridor. Somewhere behind one of the brown doors a voice on a tape-recorder, suave and careful, recited a report. The room into which he was then thrust had an uncurtained, barred window that looked out over rooftops, drainpipes, a church steeple and chimneys. A flock of pigeons flew against the sky in untidy formation, and the sky was flat blue and hazeless. Before the window was a big desk with two telephones, neatly-arranged stacks of foolscap covered in writing, buff files, a pen rack, little trays of pins and paperclips.

The sportsman said, '*Hier is hy, majoor.* Here he is, major.'

'Let him sit down,' the Major, who was sitting behind the desk, said.

He was broad and seemed to be constructed of a series of pink ovals: balding head and fat oval face, fat neck that topped curving shoulders which formed the upper curve of the big oval that was his rotund trunk: he could have been an advertisement for good cheer. He was in shirtsleeves, and the hands which emerged from the starched cuffs were pink and plump and oval. Only his eyes were small and round and shiny, like two glass beads; small, bright, conscienceless eyes. Yet when he spoke his voice took on a friendly, sympathetic tone, like a doctor advising a patient.

3

'Ah, *ja*, we know you,' he said. 'You must believe that we have known you for some time, but until now we have not bothered. But certain things have happened, is it not? So now we have become interested.' The small, prissy mouth smiled, but his eyes belied the assumed air of bonhomie. There was a defect in the disguise; the mask did not conceal all.

'I do not understand the ingratitude of your people,' he went on. 'Look what we, our Government, have done for your people. We have given you nice jobs, houses, education. Education, *ja*. Take education for instance. We have allowed you people to get education, your own special schools, but you are not satisfied. No, you want more than what you get. I have heard that some of your young people even want to learn mathematics. What good is mathematics to you? You see, you people are not the same as we are. We can understand these things, mathematics. We know the things which are best for you. We have gone far to help you, do things for you. Yet you want to be like the Whites. It's impossible. You want this country to be like Ghana, the Congo. Look what they did in the Congo. You people will never be able to govern anything. But we understand that you must have certain things, rights, so we have arranged for you to have the things you need, under our supervision.'

The rotund body squirmed in the chair; the plump, pink hands were extended open on the desk in a gesture of appeal. The little blue eyes even looked sad, or was it a trick of light? The prisoner looked at him and thought, he believes he is making a speech, pleading with me to understand. For an instant he wanted to laugh, but the Major went on and he listened again, with curiosity, to the words.

'Yes, you see, man, we have granted you all this.' The oval hands motioned towards the bars, the buff files, the paperclips. 'But people like you are never satisfied. You want to mislead your people, just like you have been misled by certain other people – clever people, priests, lawyers, Communists.'

'Jews,' the sportsman added, speaking for the first time. He

4

looked furiously at the prisoner, as if affronted that the Major should have to condescend to educating this animal.

'We want you people to accept what we are doing,' the Major said. 'But some, like you for instance, think they are smart. Nobody believes you, but you keep on. Now it is my task to stop it, you see. It is my duty to destroy your organization. Already you people are on your knees; soon you will be on your bellies. Soon we will stamp you out altogether. We know all about you. You see, man, it is no use, because we have people working for us, for the good of your people, and they co-operate with us.

'Now, we know that you are in charge of a section in these parts. You are in touch with others, like that fellow who got away. But we will soon have him too. I want you to tell me who that other one is, his name, where he lives, etcetera etcetera. Everything. I want you to tell us the names of all who work with you, where you meet, and so on. Who is your contact with the central committee or the high command – is that what you call it? If you speak now, you will be okay, you will save yourself a lot of trouble. If you don't talk now, you will later on, but then all the trouble you go through, and the damage, will have been for nothing. You know we need not bring you to court; we can hold you indefinitely, merely on suspicion.'

The small blue eyes scanned the prisoner like the points of surgical flashlights, bright and without expression. The prisoner smiled a little and said: 'But if, as you say, we are wrong and only making trouble, and that nobody believes us, why are you so concerned with us?'

The sportsman shouted angrily: 'We don't want to hear that nonsense. Just tell the Major what he wants to know.'

The prisoner ignored him and said to the Major, 'You want me to co-operate. You have shot my people when they have protested against unjust treatment; you have torn people from their homes, imprisoned them, not for stealing or murder, but for not having your permission to live. Our children live in rags and die

5

of hunger. And you want me to co-operate with you? It is impossible.'

There was a dryness in his throat and he was surprised at himself for being able to say these words so directly to the man behind the desk. His cheek burned where the skin had been scraped off; he felt harrassed, lonely, hunted, but he carried with him a sense of great injustice and a desperate pride.

'Shit,' the sportsman said. 'You're not at a bloody public meeting now. We'll make you piss blood, you baboon.'

'No,' the Major said. 'He is no baboon. He is one of the "big shots", the "top brass" in these parts.' You could hear the quotation marks click into place around the slang terms. Beyond the window the flat blue sky was now hazy with the growing heat of the late summer. The prisoner wondered when he would see the sky again.

He said: 'You are going to torture me, maybe kill me. But that is the only way you and your people can rule us. You shoot and kill and torture because you cannot rule in any other way a people who reject you. You are reaching the end of the road and going downhill towards a great darkness, so you must take a lot of people with you, because you are selfish and greedy and afraid of the coming darkness...'

'I don't want to hear your rubbish,' the Major said. 'Tell me what I want to know, or I'll have your balls out.'

The prisoner had been expecting the Major's total transformation from assumed benignity to abrupt threats, so it did not come as a surprise. All that sugar wasted, he thought. Now he prepared himself for violence.

'I have already spoken,' he said. He was afraid, but clung to his pride and the sense of injustice. That's the last speech I'll make, he thought; the last.

The young one and the sportsman dragged him to his feet again and rushed him out, giving him little chance to walk. They hustled him along the corridor. A uniformed man opened the door at the top of the steps to a basement room. The two security men let the prisoner go and the young man kicked him

6

so that he rolled over and over down the stone steps, crying out, the handcuffs preventing him from breaking his fall.

He lay groaning at the bottom of the steps. 'Man,' the sportsman said to his companion, 'we don't want to kill him yet.' He unzipped his fly and urinated off the steps into the prisoner's face. 'That must wake him up, *ja*.' The prisoner, dripping, convulsed and retched, unable to hold back his stomach.

The two came down the steps, the sportsman doing up his trousers, and then hauled the choking prisoner up again. One got out another pair of handcuffs and snapped one end to the pair already holding his wrists. They thrust him, retching, over to a staple in the wall and clicked the other end of the manacles to it. Manacled to the staple by his wrists, his arms aloft, the prisoner choked and heaved. He was experiencing an awful sensation of asphyxiation and horrifying doom. Far away, he was suddenly a child again and he had fallen into the dam and was drowning, smelly water filling his nose, while his companions ran up and down the bank in terror.

The two detectives removed their jackets and the sportsman hit him in the stomach and then began to batter him mercilessly with his fists. It was like working at a bag in a gymnasium. When one was tired, the other took over. The prisoner fought for breath and struggled to avoid the blows. He could smell his own vomit and the detective's urine on his clothes. Strength drained from his body like water from a burst bottle. The young one drew his revolver and struck at the prisoner's writhing shins with the barrel. Pain sprang through his legs with the stab of skinning-knives. His legs went numb and he hung by the manacles while the young man smacked him with the pistol barrel. He cried out in pain – pain from his legs, from his battered body, from the manacled wrists by which he dangled.

The one in the sports clothes said, blowing hard after his efforts: 'There will be more to come, you *donder*. You will talk.'

7

CHAPTER ONE

In the municipal park the trees made rough patterns on the brown gravel of the pathways. They were oak trees, and brown acorns left over from the winter lay in the conduits along the sides of the paths; the leaves, sparse now in the late summer mottled the grass and gravel, curling like snippets of dead skin in the hot sun. Among the trees were cultivated patches in the billiard-table lawns, the patches were grown with various plants and little sticks pinned with labels in front of each gave their names in English and Latin. Now and then a squirrel came face-down from the oaks and darted into the forest of carefully-tended flowers. In the centre of the park was an ornamental pond with water-lilies patching its transparent brown surface, and reddish-goldfish jerking nervously below them. Beyond the pond the Portuguese explorer, who had been the first European to land on that part of the world, gazed granitely across the oak trees towards the bay, his cassock-like robe and hewn hair speckled by the pigeons, his stone eyes made cynical by a trick of the sunlight. Behind him a maze of pathways led to the museum and the open-air restaurant: Whites only. Beyond all that the edge of the city clambered upward in steps of wealthy thoroughfares to the green foothills and the blue-grey face of the mountain.

Beatie Adams knew the municipal park well. She knew every pathway, every bench, every hothouse where they kept the orchids and other exotic flowers. She knew which were the warmest spots as the sun travelled across the brown gravel, grey concrete, green grass and trees. She knew the park because she brought the baby there for his outing each morning and again after lunch during the warm months, and she had been doing it for almost two years now.

Today she was out in the late morning sunshine again, pushing the baby carriage before her: stout and near middle age, wearing the white cap and washed-out white smock, with their appearance of clinical sterility, as if they branded her with her own childlessness, but yet bestowed her with authority to raise the offspring of others. She kept to the sunlight, circling the mottled stains of the shadows wherever she could, enjoying the heat on her broad tan-coloured, pleasant face. In the cart the infant, pink, golden-haired and healthy, dozed under the blue plastic canopy. A squirrel flashed across the pathway ahead of her, streaking for the ornamental scrub on the other side of the path, and a flock of pigeons, disturbed by the sudden rush, rose from the gravel, some of them whirring into the branches of the oaks, others heading across the park towards the neo-classic art gallery.

There were other people in the park: office messengers in uniform suits taking a short-cut towards the centre of the city; anonymous men and women crunching along the brown tracks; white pensioners dozing on the green benches; an old man with a spiked stick searching for discarded lunch packets and ice cream wrappers. Beatie Adams strolled along the bright path-ways, searching for a 'Non-White' seat. The baby slept peace-fully under the canopy.

She found a place at last. Her favourite spots were all occu-pied, but this one was good enough. One man occupied the end of the slatted bench and he appeared to be sleeping. She sat down at the other end, made sure that the carriage was properly braked, and relaxed back in the comforting warmth. She would sit there for a half-hour, she thought, and then make her way slowly back home. Home was a room in the servants' quarters off the backyard of a big, pink and white house near the park. It was comfortable enough: a single bed with a candlewick cover, some store furniture – discarded when the missus had purchased a new suite – a picture of her mother in a cheap frame and another of a country scene, bottles of lotion on the

9

dresser, and a motley collection of paraphernalia which all went into making life liveable.

The baby woke up and wailed, rubbing his eyes sleepily with a clenched fist.

Beatie Adams said, 'There, there, there,' soothingly and rearranged the light coverlet over the infant.

She looked up again and found the man at the end of the bench watching her.

'Did the baby wake you?'

'Oh, it's okay. I must have been dozing.'

'The sun makes you sleepy,' she said.

'Yah.' He yawned into a fist. 'Excuse me. Been up all night.' He glanced at his wrist. He was holding a parcel wrapped in brown paper on his lap, and a rolled newspaper. Sleepy, copper brown eyes like moist farthings, and a mouth with a longish upper-lip smiled at her. There was a small scar under the left eye, on the cheekbone, and the delicate, almost girlish chin and jaw-line were smudged with overnight stubble. On the whole the face had an air of agelessness; he could have been twenty-five or forty-five, it was difficult to say. The brown suit was cheap, but not so cheap that it wrinkled permanently, and he wore a lighter brown shirt, the collar gone limp, and a maroon patterned necktie. There was reddish-brown dust from the gravelled pathway on his tan brogues.

'Yes. He just woke up.'

'Like me.' The brown eyes were weary, but he flashed the teeth under the long upper-lip.

She laughed a little shyly, and then looked away at the baby. She wasn't used to making conversation with strangers. It was the left-over of a warning given her years ago when she had left the countryside to take up work as a domestic. Take care of yourself, don't trust those city people, her mother had warned. It had stuck with her somehow, like the country accent, in spite of the relentless attacks of urban life. She remembered it now, and thought with mild bitterness, maybe that's why I'm still single.

'You come here every day?'

For a moment she thought he intended trying to make a date, but decided it was just friendly conversation. He did not look the forward type.

'In the nice weather, yes.'

'I reckon you do more for the baby than its mother.'

'Oh, I like looking after children. His mother goes out in the day. His father's a traveller – kind of petrol company.'

'Yah. It's like that with them. You raise the kids, change the nappies, give them the bottle. When they grow up then they forget it and become part of the rest looking down on us.'

'Yes, I suppose so.'

'From up country?'

'Oh, a long time already. Seventeen years.'

'I was born here.' He gestured with a hand at the pigeons, the skyline of city blocks, an old man sleeping in the sun and breathing stentoriously through a wet, pink, toothless mouth. 'I been working in service all the time.'

'We all good enough to be servants. Because we're black they think we good enough just to change their nappies.'

She said, hesitantly, wondering whether it would be the right answer, 'That's life, isn't it?'

It wasn't, she could feel, because he said, 'Life? Why should it be our life? We're as good or bad as they are.'

'Yes, I reckon so. But what can us people do?'

The brown eyes smiled. They were red-rimmed from lack of sleep, but not angry in spite of the bitter tone he had used. He rubbed the short overnight stubble on his jaw with a long brown finger. 'There are things people can do,' his voice was not sleepy, 'I'm not saying a person can change it tomorrow or next year. But even if you don't get what you want today, soon, it's a matter of pride, dignity. You follow me?'

'It's so hopeless. You only get into trouble.'

He yawned and shrugged. 'Trouble. There's always trouble.' He spoke as if trouble was something he experienced all the time, but trouble was a stranger to her. He was a man of the world, while she was safe within the fortress in the backyard, with the cast-off furniture and the picture of her mother. If she knew trouble, it came in the form of admonishments that the baby had a nappy-rash or that there was dust on the sideboard.

The noon gun boomed on the hill beyond the city and the clock in the City Hall tower began to strike across the rooftops. The man looked at his wrist-watch, pulling back the sleeve of his jacket, and yawned again. 'Excuse me,' he smiled. 'Late nights. I have to go and see somebody.'

'You shouldn't stay up so late,' she said jocularly and had visions of drinking and dancing with carefree women, while he laughed, getting to his feet. The brown suit was wrinkled and it did not fit very well at the back: the kind you bought ready-made and paid for in weekly instalments. He was fairly tall and the ageless face was not unpleasant. She thought it was the kind of face that would last a life-time, without growing old: a not-too-ugly carving out of good teakwood. There was a carving on the sideboard in the house where she worked and the master had said it was valuable.

The man said, 'Well, so long. Sorry we can't talk some more. Keep an eye on the baby.'

'Bye.' She bent over to adjust the light blanket around the sleeping infant and when she looked up the man was disappearing among the oak trees. She noticed that he had left his newspaper behind on the park bench, but it was too late to call him back. He was gone and where she had last seen him walking there was an old gentleman leaning forward to feed nuts to a squirrel, and the top of the statue of Rhodes pointing north towards the segregated lavatories: Yonder lies your hinterland.

She picked up the newspaper and unfolded it, telling herself she would spend another fifteen minutes in the sun before going back to prepare the baby's feed. The printer's ink was smeared along the folds and the paper frayed, as if nervous hands had rolled it tight, gripping it all the time. She thought

12

vaguely of a long brown finger, and scanned the front page. A woman accused of murdering her husband was to appear in court that morning: Bainsburg Murder, Woman Appears Today, the headline stated. Suddenly Beatie Adams remembered a country station, milk cans, a sheep pen, a coloured man in a railway cap sweeping the platform as her train pulled slowly past, carrying her towards the city, years ago. Surely, she thought, it couldn't be *that* place. There was a picture of a wood and metal house, horse-drawn wagons, and corrugated iron fences. A uniformed policeman stood self-consciously on the verandah at the shut door of the house, one hand on his gun holster. In another picture a woman's face in grey half-tone, wearing a hat like a dark halo, obtruded into the smudged report: Mrs Katerina Zuidenhout. Beatie Adams wondered how people could be so nasty as to go around murdering each other. It was a world not included in a succession of servants' rooms. She flapped the newspaper at a pigeon which had alighted on the canopy of the baby carriage and it fluttered away, made a circle of the path, and then headed in the direction of the museum.

Walking past the entrance to the museum, Beukes was reminded of an appointment he had kept there four years past. It had been summer then, too, and he recollected with surprise that he had been up all night on that occasion as well. For a time it was like re-living the past; a colour slide repeated on a screen.

The entrance of the museum had been chill, in spite of the summer weather. Somehow there was always an atmosphere of coldness at a museum; an atmosphere of refrigerated preservation. He saw again, in his mind's eye, the line of hushed children, accompanied by their schoolmaster, tiptoeing under the chill arch into the lobby; a little boy nervously holding a packet of sandwiches and an orange while the schoolmaster shush-shushed at them. Strolling into the dim lobby that squeaked under his feet, he had felt the eyes of a uniformed attendant scan him briefly from behind a newspaper. Out of the corner of his eye he had seen, behind the glass of a cubicle, a blue uniform cap and the word 'Strike'. For a moment he had wondered whether he could be challenged as not looking like somebody interested in the stuffed animals, the monkey foetus in a glass jar, and the crushed flea behind a magnifying glass. But he had gone on into the dimness, past the medieval weaponry, the headsman's swords and axes, the old-fashioned muskets and breastplates, and up the broad polished stairway towards the upper floor.

It had been sunnier there. The light splashed in through big windows illuminating the glass eyes of the leopards, lions and baboons like faulty radio valves. He had been alone, a stranger in a lost, dead world. A bull elephant, stuffed and motionless, had lurked behind a glass case full of various kinds of monkey frozen on imitation branches, the white name-tag pinned beneath each pose adding to the grotesquerie. For a few minutes he had lost his way and had wandered amid sarcophagi and the plaster heads of pharoahs until he had found the anthropological section. There Bushmen had hunted with bows and tiny arrows behind glass; red-yellow dwarfs with peppercorn hair and beady eyes. Beukes had thought sentimentally that they were the first to fight. He had walked silently past the still ochre figures crouched over cooking pots and ostrich shell water-bottles, and there, in a rectangle of dust-speckled yellow light, he had found Isaac.

Issac had been sitting alone on the edge of a polished wooden bench like a nervous newcomer in church, his hands clasped in his lap, waiting for the service to begin. He had looked up with a start at the sound of Beuke's footfalls, and had grabbed at the arm of the seat.

'Boo!' Beukes had smiled. 'It's only me. How's it, chum?'

'You gave me a fright,' Isaac had said smiling back. 'I reckoned . . .'

'Don't worry,' Beukes had said, sitting down. 'They're not looking for us yet.'

'How do you know?' Isaac had gazed around the big room

14

with its glass cases and polished floors, as if he expected an ambush.

Beukes had yawned and said, 'I phoned all over. No raids, no searches. What's new?'

Isaac had short curly hair, a light complexion and prominent pink ears. There had been a faint reddish down on his cheeks and his eyes bulged a little, giving him a permanent look of slight surprise. He had always been a little nervous and his blunt-fingered hands had plucked at the knees of his trousers. He had worn a long khaki dustcoat over his clothes. 'So far, so good,' he had said. 'The three I got together in my district are still willing to work. Dunno what's going to happen when the cops start buggering around. There's Paul . . .'

'No names, no pack drill,' Beukes had told him. 'Forget the cops for a while, though.'

'Some of our people are going to get shit scared,' Isaac had replied. He had peered about again. 'Are we alone?'

'Sure, man. Nobody comes to a museum this time of day.'

'How's Frances?'

'Ah, all right. Getting big.'

'Christ,' Isaac had said, 'she's like that and you're not worried?'

Beukes had yawned. 'Haven't slept. Bloody committee meeting. Who says I'm not worried? I got a wife who's in the family way for the first time. We got a strike coming off in a few weeks. Just now the cops will start farting around. You reckon I'm not worried? You bloody well right I'm worried. But what's the use of worrying? Nothing will get done that way.' He had grinned at Isaac. 'What's the use of worrying? Pack up your troubles and smile, smile, smile.'

'Reckon you wish this all happened at another time,' Isaac had said as he gazed at a reddish figure who was pointing at a track in the sand on the floor of a glass case.

'So let's keep on the bright side, hey. Let's get down to business.' Beukes had placed his satchel case on the bench between them.

15

'Where'd you duck last night?'

'I didn't. We had a meeting all night and I didn't go home. Never mind that.' He had stretched his legs and yawned again. 'Can a guy smoke here?'

'No,' Isaac had replied, 'better not.'

'Okay. Now you got three. That's smart. First thing is we got to give them some work to do. I'll be getting the leaflets tonight and they'll be delivered to you. There'll be transport, but it's not my department. The stuff's got to be dished out to-morrow. Some for the factories, some house to house. Your gang got factory connections?'

'One of them is in a clothing faktry,' Isaac had told him. 'The other two are just round and about.'

Beukes had wondered what round and about meant, but he had just said, 'Okay. The factory bloke got to take some in. Leave them around on machines, in the canteen. Warn him not to be caught doing it. We don't want him flung out on his ear, or handed over this early.'

'What about meetings?'

'Well, we had the big meeting yesterday to launch the thing. No more hullabaloo, just small meetings round and about.' He had smiled at his own use of Isaac's phrase. 'Difficult at a factory now. Somebody might call the cops. We got to concentrate on houses. Now your gang's got to dish the other leaflets out house to house. At night, it's best.'

'Sure.'

'At the same time you got to try and find people in your district ready to have meetings in their homes.'

'We'll scout around.'

'And about,' Beukes had grinned again. 'Maybe one of your three.'

'I'll talk to them.'

'That's for a start. The same thing's happening other places. We'll spread out from there.'

Isaac had said, 'I hope so. You reckon this thing will come off?

16

'Am I a fortune teller?' Beukes had asked. 'It depends on the tempo we can keep up and the initial interest we can work on. We mustn't slacken.'

Isaac had stared at the figures in the glass cases, his prominent eyes serious, for a moment no longer surprised. 'They been having their own bloody way too long. I hope we can give them a great scare this time, it'll help the people, too.' He had looked at Beukes. 'Don't worry, Buke, we'll give it stick.'

Beukes had said kindly, 'I know you will, Ike.'

'When they get cracking they'll be after you blokes, the ones they know.'

'Ah, we'll give them a run before it's over.' A pigeon had alighted on a window-sill and its rustle had come into the silent room. The still figures of the first people had not been disturbed; an outstretched hand still held a trapped hare by the ears. Then Beukes had said, 'Now remember, do things properly and don't get caught. They don't know you and your gang. You'll get the leaflets.'

Isaac had grinned, 'It's you that's worrying now.'

'I worry all the time,' Beukes had said. 'I'm a great worrier.'

Then Isaac had asked, 'Is that all now? I got to get back to work. Got to do the post early.'

'Okay, then. I'll see you tonight. It will be late-ish though.'"

'Hmmm. Look, hey, in case everything is locked up, just leave the stuff on the back doorstep.'

'Will it be okay?'

'Yeh, don't worry.' Isaac had got up, 'I got to run.'

'Right-o. You go first.'

'Be seeing you, Buke.'

Beukes had watched him go off, shoes squeaking on the polished floor, his long khaki coat drooping like limp wings behind him, then he had disappeared among the still hunters holding their primitive bows in petrified readiness. When Isaac had gone, Beukes had risen and had gone off in the same direction. In the Egyptian room an old couple had looked up from a collection of scarabs as he passed and had then continued whispering over the carved beetles. He had caught the whispered word, 'luck', and had known that it couldn't be meant for him, but he had smiled all the same, going downstairs with his satchel, his eyes feeling gritty with lack of sleep.

Now passing the museum Beukes remembered all this. The shadowed doorway was unchanged, except that now a notice proclaimed separate days for Whites and Non-Whites. He emerged from the botanical gardens into a quiet, shadowy street. A block of expensive flats towered at one corner, all glass and mosaic-work, and a little way ahead a taxi-cab dropped its passengers in front of an hotel. A woman with a decorated face and wide brimmed hat like a cartwheel, said, 'You pay, Ethel. I hope we're not too late ...' while a uniformed porter hurried forward, hands extended as if he was about to catch something.

Beukes went past the hotel and up a short, steep street, coming into a thoroughfare of cheap, forlorn-looking shops. A row of milk-cans stood on the wet pavement outside a dairy and under an awning a girl swept the sidewalk in front of a dusty window that announced shabbily: *Curtaining, It's A Bargain At 29c A Yard*. He walked unhurriedly but watchfully along the footpath, past the windows under the blistered balconies, carrying the parcel with his pyjamas and toilet kit, and thought, you never know where they are, but who would say anything serious was happening? Life went on: it was lunchtime and a group of workers sat at the kerbside playing draughts, two factory girls in blue smocks and caps looked at dresses in another window, a trolley-bus swayed by, heading half-empty towards the centre of the city. Ahead he saw two policemen wearing guns and khaki uniforms, but he didn't bother about them; the secret police wore no uniforms.

He turned aside into a residential street drenched with sun and flanked by rows of houses that went irregularly up the steep slope to the foot of Signal Hill. A row of cars, most of them belonging to the local shopkeepers, paraded down the middle of the street; an old man in a fez dozed on a high verandah under a line of washing that hung like bunting. Beukes climbed the cement steps in front of one of the houses and saw, with some relief, that the front door was open.

In the entrance passageway a hallstand displayed a navy-blue raincoat like a drab and dusty flag hung out long ago and forgotten, but the straw hat with the colourful band belonged to this season, like the suitcase that blocked the way across the bright linoleum.

Beukes was about to knock when Arthur Bennett came out of the bedroom off the passageway, holding a child's bucket and spade and a plastic groundsheet saying, 'What must I do with this?' He saw Beukes in the doorway and looked surprised. The look of surprise changed rapidly into a nervous bonhomie and he cried, 'Buke, you bugger, there you are.'

Beukes said, smiling bleakly, 'Hullo, you old crook.'

A woman's voice called from somewhere inside the house, 'Who's there? If it's the milky . . .'

'It's Buke,' Bennett called back and flushed nervously. 'Beukes. You know Beukes.' To Beukes he said: 'Come on in, pal. Mind the case.'

He led the way into a region of linoleum, polished chairs and a dining-table with a big brass vase shaped like a cooking-pot. One was reminded of jokes about cannibals and missionaries. A low stuffed settee and heavy armchairs with circular, gleaming wooden armrests were crowded along one wall. There were starched, crocheted table centres and a display cabinet full of miniature bottles which had once contained sample liqueurs and soft drinks. There was some more brass: ashtrays, a set of fire-irons (although there was no grate), and two candlesticks which would have been at home on an altar.

Bennett said, 'We just got back, pal. Had a helluva time at the beach.'

Beukes was about to ask, 'The coloured beach?' But instead he said, 'I was here Saturday morning as arranged. It was all locked up.'

Bennett flushed and said, embarrassed, 'Sorry, old pal. Nelly reckoned we should leave Friday night instead. Women always changing their minds the last minute.' He put the beachware down beside a bookcase containing nothing but a set of new-looking encyclopaedias, and pulled a face, jerking a thumb in the direction of another room, whispering, 'She didn't like it. Sorry.'

As if she had overheard, the woman's voice called out, 'I don't want any bladdy trouble.'

Bennett said again, 'Sorry, pal. Did you find a place to doss down?'

'Oh, I managed,' Beukes said, and thought, you hypocritical bastards.

The woman came out of the room and said, curtly, 'Hullo' to Beukes, and to Bennett: 'We better finish unpacking before the child wake up. I haven't got all bladdy day.' She was small and fine boned and pretty as a garden snake.

Bennett flushed and grinned at Beukes. He was a short man, younger than Beukes, but already bald, his brown skull under the few thin hairs, shiny as the furniture and brass in the room. He had anxious, harrassed eyes that fought to maintain the disguise of bonhomie, but it kept slipping like a badly-glued moustache in a school play. He gestured with bony hands. 'Do you want to sit down?'

Beukes looked at him, feeling a little sorry for the harrassed fellow. He said, 'No, don't bother. But if you can let me brush my teeth and shave . . .'

'Oh, sure, oh, sure. That's no trouble.' He sounded relieved that he could do a small favour to compensate for a more important failure. 'This way. Through there.' He gestured vaguely towards the kitchen. 'We just got back a little while ago. Had to drop the old lady. You go ahead, Buke.'

In the bathroom Beukes shaved quickly and angrily, brushed his teeth, using some of the toothpaste he found on a shelf, and splashed his face. He dried it on one of their towels and wrapped his shaving kit and brush once more with the pyjamas. When he came into the other room he said, with a little malice, 'They going to declare this place White. You'll be pushed out into the *bundu*.'

Bennett looked solemn. 'I heard so. They always doing this kind of thing to us.'

The woman came in and said, 'There's no time for politics now, Arty. You got a lot to do, hey.' She disappeared into the kitchen.

Beukes ignored her, saying, 'That poor bloke in Sea Point went and hanged himself when they had to move, after living there God knows how long.'

Bennett said, 'Yes,' glumly.

Beukes jabbed at him with words, punishing the harrassed bald man, and enjoying it: 'And you, you bastard, you can't even lift a finger. A bloke asks you to give him a place to sleep while you're away for a weekend at the beach, but no – you got to promise him it's okay and then you bladdy well sneak off.'

Bennett said feebly, 'Nelly was afraid of trouble.'

'What trouble? They don't know you. All it meant was I'd stay a couple of nights here and then I'd be off again the time you got back.'

'Somebody might of seen you.'

Beukes said gleefully, 'Like right now, hey?'

Bennett looked shocked. He put a hand on his bald pate. 'Oh, God.'

From the other room his wife cried: 'When are you going to stop talking?'

Beukes said, 'Don't worry. Nobody that mattered saw me.' He grinned at Bennett with the long upper-lip. 'Thanks for the wash and brush-up.' He began to move towards the passageway, the other man following him, looking worried. The bony hands waved about like faulty signals. 'Sorry, pal.'

'Sorry? What the hell you mean sorry?'

Bennett flushed again and then put a hand in a trouser pocket. He said, 'Look, here's ten bob. A donation.' He displayed the note nervously and glanced back over his shoulder. His eyes pleaded. 'You know how it is, Buke. Nelly's scared.

She ain't mean. Just scared. People talk. They got informers everywhere. You can't even trust your best friend. Here. It's a donation, likely.'

Beukes looked at the note, then shrugged. He was sorry he had hurt the small, bald man. He said, 'Keep it. You don't have to buy your way out.' Bennett followed him to the front door. 'How's the boys up north doing?'

'They wiped out a bunch of soljers,' Beukes told him.

'That's the stuff,' Bennett said smiling. But at the front door he was nervous again. 'You sure nobody saw you come in, Buke?'

Beukes looked at him, grinned and then shook his head sadly. He went down the steps with his paper parcel, into the hot sunlight, leaving the other man standing there nervously against the backdrop of brass ornaments and polished furniture.

CHAPTER TWO

Beukes made his way cautiously towards the lower side of the city centre where he knew a friendly taxidriver. Sleep called to him and the muscles of his legs ached. Having found Bennett's house locked and shuttered that past Saturday morning, he had thought of returning the same night and breaking in to stay the weekend as arranged, but had decided against it. He imagined himself poised on the back-yard wall surrounded by threatening neighbours and the police; it made him smile. So he had made his way into the expensive White district on the mountainside above the city — a quiet and respectable part where the police did not patrol frequently. There he had spent two nervous and sleepless nights in a pretty gully, among pines and perfumed undergrowth, using his pyjamas as a groundsheet instead of sleeping attire. He smiled again, in spite of fatigue, at the thought of wearing pyjamas among the daisies and pine needles. He could have gone direct to the other place, but you had to stick to the arrangements: security had to be as good as the enemy's, if that was possible. They had the whole organization of the authoritarian state ranged against you.

At the foot of the main street traffic splashed in from the seafront suburbs and purled away among the mixture of Victorian and modern buildings of the city centre, then re-treated again in all directions, back towards Sea Point, Camps Bay, or inland.

For a while Beukes was in a crowd on the sidewalk. You could get lost in a crowd; in an alleyway or alone on a street you were conspicuous. Yet he felt his heart beat uncomfortably, and his eyes panned across the faces of passers-by. A bellboy with a black face under a pillbox hat opened the glass doors of a big hotel for a guest, and his white-gloved hands released a trickle of tourist sounds: the clink of glasses; a woman's voice saying nasally, '... must come to Los Angeles some day ...' soft music from the dim futuristic cocktail lounge where the Indian stewards moved skilfully among the tables. The bell-boy stood guard at the doorway to forbidden luxury.

Nearby was the huge, brand-new modern railway station (the section for Blacks was a mile away). At the tourist bureau a sleek, streamlined coach was taking on a line of White passengers in front of the gay posters of lions, golf courses and sunny beaches. Down the Boulevarde the glass and marble squares and rectangles formed cubist arms, open to welcome the newcomer at the waterfront where the liners and merchantmen bobbed gently behind a hedge of cranes. Some time ago somebody had painted a sign in bleeding words on a blank wall facing the harbour, and sandblasting could not obliterate the outlines of the heavy letters: *You Are Now Entering The Police State.*

The taxidriver wore a brown leather cap. He was slouched down behind the wheel, reading a paperback. The fingers that turned one of the pages were short and thick; the rough nails wore rims of grease and tiny outcrops of black down stood out between the knuckles. Stooping to look through the window, Beukes saw the hands and the violent cover of the book: A naked woman and a man pointing a gun. As if we don't have enough of that, he thought.

He said quietly, 'Howdy, wise guy.'

The driver looked up from his book. He was wearing dark green sunglasses which gave the impression of two holes cut out of his face. He smiled widely, showing two gold teeth, and said, '*Boeta* Buke, you old *skelm*, howzit?'

'Okay,' Beukes said. 'Everything right with you?'

'Fix up.'

The driver leaned over and unlocked the door and Beukes climbed into the back of the car while the gangster novel was stowed into the cubbyhole. The car ground into life and Beukes, sitting on the edge of the seat, said, 'Tommy's joint,

24

hey?' He thought sleepily, it's like a bloody gangster picture itself. Life had become mysterious rides, messages left in obscure places, veiled telephone conversations. The torture chambers and the third degree had been transferred from celluloid strips in segregated cinemas to the real world which still hung on to its outward visible signs of peace: the shoppers innocently crowding the sidewalks, the racing results, the Saturday night parties, the act of love.

Beukes remembered the electrode burns on the hands of prisoners. Behind the picture of normality the cobwebs and grime of a spider reality lay hidden. Men and women disappeared from sight, snatched into the barred cells of the security police, into the square rooms with the Public Works Department teacups and the thin-lipped, red-faced men with mocking eyes and brutal minds, into the world of clubbed fists and electric instruments of torture, the days and nights of sleeplessness, the screams.

The taxidriver said, 'You's awright, *Boeta* Buke?'

'So-so.'

'I don't know what this ——ing country is coming to.' The driver adjusted the sunblind in front of him. 'My goose, she work already in this faktry twelve years, now she tell me she must give up her place as supervisor of the conveyor belt to some white bitch to take over. You got to have a white person tell you do this and do that.'

'Going on a long time,' Beukes said.

'*Ja*, I know. But when it happen to you personal or to somebody close, well, it make *mos* a bogger sit up and think.'

They swept past the waterfront and the railroad yards. Beukes lay back in his seat, low, peering out over the edge of the window, watching the passing traffic and looking back through the rear window now and again. He wanted to drop off to sleep. Now that he was in the car, sleep crowded against him and he felt hot and weary, but he knew he had to keep awake. You learned to be on the look-out, unless you were absolutely under cover, a fox in its hole, a lizard under a rock, but even then you were unsure. They might be near, they might be nowhere or everywhere, you never really could tell.

He was not really listening to the driver's chatter, he was too tired to think or talk, but he said, 'Yes' and 'No' now and then.

They left the waterfront, climbed a fly-over bridge and entered a cramped, oily district full of factories, warehouses and garages then crossed the secondary suburban main road and climbed into the back of the slum area. The sector had the look of a town cleared after a battle. Whole blocks had disappeared, leaving empty, flattened lots surrounded by battered survivors.

'. . . whole ——ing place is going,' the driver was saying.

'Yep,' Beukes said sleepily.

'They going to do it up again for white people,' the driver complained. '*They* not going to get no rag-tag warrens. Blocks of flats, new houses, I reckon. Said so in the papers. I don't understand it, we people been living *mos* here awready a hundred years.'

A pile of banana crates stood against a wall with a scabby sign that said 'Bombay Fruit Produce', and two children in ragged clothes searched the gutters. A woman with unkempt hair shook a blanket from a tenement window as if she was signalling to somebody far across the terrain of empty squares and isolated buildings. Here and there the voices of defiance cried silently across the stretches of pockmarked walls: *Down With Racist Tyranny; Free Our Leaders*.

They were in the main street of a ghost town. Along the shadowy pavements under the old iron and wood balconies shopwindows, boarded up when their owners had abandoned trade in the wake of the general exodus, stared with blinded eyes out into the grimy, sunlit throughfare. The shopping crowds of the past had dwindled noticeably and now people moved along the sidewalks, past the rows of shabby shopfronts, like the survivors of a holocaust. Over the patched and mended balconies odd washlines still hung like the rigging of ghost ships, and frayed trousers dangled in the sun like a signal for

help. There was a small crowd around the cinema, rotating for-
lornly under the billboards that made a gaudy montage against
the background of greys and blistered browns. Here and there
tiny cafes clung to precarious business with the fingernails of
hope, like the foxholes of a last-ditch stand, dust gathering on
the stale menu cards. The fishmarket was deserted, the stalls
shuttered, and two men in undervests sat on an upturned pack-
ing-case and smoked idly while they perspired in the yellow
sunlight.

It was hot in the car and Beukes had loosened his necktie
and collar. He could feel the perspiration in his armpits, like
blood down his breastbone, and his eyes ached with fatigue.

The driver was asking, 'You reckon we ever going to win,
Buke?'

'Huh? What?'

'You reckon we ever going to win?'

'We'll win,' Beukes told him, yawning, wanting to fall asleep.
He wished the driver would stop talking; right then he did not
give a damn about politics, the resistance, the revolution; all he
wanted to do was get some sleep.

Then they turned into a narrow street hemmed in by old
tenements and a mosque, and the car pulled up by the kerb.
'Here's it,' the driver said. Then, 'Something goes on down
there.' His voice was suddenly low and taut with caution.

A little way down the street a small crowd had gathered
around a pile of old furniture and a broken-down, horse-drawn
barrow onto which two men were loading household effects.
Beukes and the taxidriver watched for a while.

'Just somebody moving house,' Beukes said.

The driver relaxed and then leaned back to unlock the door
for Beukes. 'You know *mos* the way up.'

'*Ja*, I know the place.'

'Well, okay then Buke, good luck, hey.'

'So long, take it easy, man. And thanks, hey.'

The driver smiled with his gold teeth and sunglasses, saluted
with a thick hand, then drove away. Beukes stood on the

27

cracked, sundrenched sidewalk with the sleepiness, the smell of his own sweat, and the brown paper parcel. He watched the small crowd down the street for a moment before entering the building.

An old woman was sitting in an old deckchair in the middle of the crowd amongst a pile of furniture. The canvas of the chair was worn where it folded around the supporting slats and the threads hung in dirty streamers, like dehydrated entrails. The canvas had been patched and stitched in places too, and a lot of the stitches had come apart, so that it looked as if the old woman would slide right through the chair at any moment. The old woman did not move. She just sat there in the middle of the crowd, with the furniture, and stared straight ahead.

An old perambulator full of old clothes and hats and worn shoes – a scuffed dancing-pump, its silver rubbed off, dangling by a crooked heel from its bent shaft – stood near her right elbow, next to the wash-stand with a cracked marble top. The stand was piled with an assortment of dusty cardboard boxes: shoe boxes, hatboxes, dressboxes, an old chocolate box with a picture of a man in Elizabethan clothes bowing over the hand of a woman in a big ruff and farthingale. Odd pieces of old furniture were packed and jumbled around the old woman: an old wardrobe with the door loose at the hinges and a cracked mirror; a chest of drawers that had once been painted, but which was now covered with ancient grime that clung to the crevices of the joints and wherever the paint had worn off. There was a kitchen table and several other smaller tables, all loaded with the accumulation of decades or generations: a fly-spotted calendar of the previous year with a curling print of a full-breasted blonde in a cowboy hat and fringed G string, and the words 'Buffalo Gal' printed along the bottom; an old-fashioned picture frame with the brown daguerreotyped face of a young man in a high collar, black string tie and laced boots posing next to a palmstand. All over were bundles and parcels of old clothes like the left-overs of a jumble sale, perched and balanced on angles and projections from the piled effects. Pots and pans with dented containers, a broken sewing machine with a split cover, a chipped wash-stand set, the handle missing from a chamberpot; basins and jars and canisters, armchairs and bedsprings, rickety bedsteads, all heaped haphazardly around the old woman, ready for loading, so that she sat in a laager of second-hand household goods.

She was a thin and gnarled old woman with ropey hair the colour of used, dirty-white knitting wool; ancient, liquid eyes stared out of the brown, clawed face with a bright, fierce dignity. Her hands, folded in the lap of her frayed coat, were hard and knotted like tangled skeins of brown cord. She wore the coat in spite of the heat, and the imitation fur collar had scaly bald patches as if it suffered from some kind of skin disease.

The shifting crowd gathered around and looked at the old woman sitting there inside the barricade of furniture, but she did not notice them, crouched there in the canvas chair with her bright, moist eyes and her impregnable dignity.

Tommy lived upstairs in one of the rooms in the same block. On the narrow, torrid staircase the smell of urine and old cooking hung on the stale, thick, groping air that touched exposed skin with a hot caress. Beukes climbed up to a corridor lined with anonymous doors. Music came, sweet and incongruous, from down the row, muted by walls, and he walked towards the sound, past ragged scolding which said, '... you reckon I'm a blerry ape to believe all that?' in a woman's scornful voice, until he reached Tommy's door.

He knocked and waited in the flannel-thick heat of the corridor. Another door opened and a man, bared to the waist, emerged carrying an overloaded rubbish bin, and headed towards the stairs leaving a wet trail of sodden papers and tea-leaves behind him. He smiled back at Beukes with an unshaven face and said, 'Blerry warm, don't I say?'

'Damn hot!' Beukes yawned and knocked again loudly, above the sound of the dance music.

The heat smothered him and he leaned his head against the door frame and shut his eyes. Instantly he dreamed that he was trudging up an escalator that was going in the opposite direction, so that he was only marking time, painfully trying to reach up towards a voice that was saying, 'Hullo, hullo, hullo, old Buke.' When he opened his eyes, there was Tommy standing in the half-open doorway.

The great white teeth grinned at him from the snub-nosed face. 'Come in, come in, Bukie, ol' chum. Man, I haven't seen you in a helluva time and when I got the message you was coming, I reckon to myself, Buke is up to his tricks again, hey.'

Beyond the kinky hair that looked like a skull cap, the music had been silenced and an old lace curtain hung like a discarded negligee over an old-fashioned porcelain jug and enamel basin under the window. Beukes noticed with relief that the window was open; even Tommy had surrendered to the weather, otherwise he would have been buttoned into his black dinner suit, for he was forever practising his ballroom steps and insisted on dressing up to do so. Now he had stripped down to his singlet, but had determinedly stuck to the pressed black trousers.

Beukes sat on the edge of the old wooden double bed that was in the room while Tommy shut the door. Then Tommy danced back towards him, his small feet moving with quick agility, the white teeth grinning like an advertisement for toothpaste.

He cried, 'Well, well, well, pally Bukie, how are you, sir?' He was gay, he was forever happy, nothing bothered him: he lived in a world of sugary saxophones and sighing strings. The other world was coincidental.

'I'm okay,' Beukes said. 'Only hot and sleepy.' He struggled out of his jacket, feeling the sleeves of his shirt clinging to his arms and smelling his own perspiration.

'Is bladdy warm, hey,' Tommy said. 'It's the last heat of the

30

summer.' He went over and lifted the tawdry lace curtain further over the jug on the table in the hope that a cooler airstream would push in through the window.

'Got any water in that jug?' Beukes asked. 'Want to wash off all this sweat.'

'Sure, sure, sure, Brother Buke.' Tommy spoke in dance rhythms whenever possible. The beat of his words shifted from foxtrot to waltz-time or to the military two-step, depending on what he was conveying. Now he spun across the floorspace towards the waterjug, splashing little droplets of moisture from his own face.

'Must you always be clowning?' Beukes asked him sleepily.

'Be a clown, be a clown, be a clown,' Tommy sang and poured water into the basin. Then he changed to a slower, sadder blues of seriousness. 'How's your business, ol' Bukie?' He knew vaguely that Beukes's 'business' involved handing out printed papers during the night, calling on people to strike, even being arrested. Enquiring about it was part of being polite. Give him a dance band, a light-footed woman, a smooth floor, and he was happy; he knew all the songs, the latest steps. Tommy drifted from one job to another – messenger, cleaner, dishwasher – anything, as long as there was enough at the end of the week to buy a dance record. He did not go for the wild, modern dances much; he was a dancer in the style of a past generation. An old picture of the dance-band leader, Victor Sylvester, smiled down from the wall above a radiogram that was kept as tidy as an altar. A stack of records, each one in its cover, stood on a chair.

'My business is okay,' Beukes told him. He sponged himself down at the table while Tommy hummed to himself.

'I'll hang out your shirt, Brother Buke, pally blues,' he said rhythmically. 'How about some tea for two, for me for you?'

'I'd rather have a long drink of water,' Beukes said, drying himself on a frayed towel.

From a shelf Tommy produced a tumbler and Beukes poured out some of the water from the jug. He sat on the bed in his shorts and drank the water in one gulp. 'Hell, that's better.' He looked at Tommy. 'Listen, you bogger, is it awright if I stay here awhile?'

'Don't worry about a thing, Mister Buke,' Tommy grinned toothily. 'I'm nobody's baby now.'

'What happened to that last one then? What's her name? Gwenny?'

'Ah, you know, *mos, ou* Buke, they come and they go, they come and they go.'

'Regular bladdy Casanova, hey.'

'Can I help it if they so attracted by my dancing?'

You useless bastard, Beukes thought, smiling at Tommy. But he was not useless really, was he? Tommy had known Beukes for many years and he had a sort of unconscious respect for what he considered was a crazy bloke who worried about governments and speeches instead of enjoying life. Whatever he did for this man he did out of friendship and respect, without bothering to understand what it was all about. And he did it willingly enough.

Then Beukes said, 'Listen, you bloody old clown, I want you to go somewhere for me?'

'Sure, Buke, you know me. Will it take long?'

'Not too long. I want you to go to Polsky's chemist shop.'

'Chemist? You feeling sick then?'

'No, man, it just happens to be a chemist shop. But don't ask stupid questions.'

'Okay, Buke, you know me.'

'Right. Polsky's chemist. I'll give you the address.' And he described the situation of the shop which was in an outer suburb of the city. 'I'll give you the bus fare.'

'Right, Buke. Polsky's chemist shop. I'll find it.'

'You'd better. It's important.' Beukes yawned into his fist and said, 'Well, you go there and you ask for Mister Polsky himself. Mister Polsky himself, you understand?'

'Righto, Buke.'

'Then you tell him you come for the medicine for Arthur. The medicine for Arthur.'

'I ask for Mister Polsky and ask him for the medicine for Arthur. That all?'

'Yeah, then he'll give you something and you bring it back here to me. But you got to do it straight, Tom. No buggering about on the way.'

'Don't worry, Buke. I'll go like the Chatanooga Choo Choo. Medicine for Arthur, from Mister Polsky. Will he be there? What if he isn't there?'

'He'll be there. Right, on your bicycle.' Beukes reached for his coat and found some loose change which he gave to Tommy, who was buttoning on a shirt.

'Well, I reckon you tired, Buke,' he said, 'so you just go bye-bye blues. I'll wake you up when the deep purple falls over shady garden walls.' He laughed happily and picked up the basin from the table to empty it somewhere outside the room before setting out.

Beukes lay back on the bed and shut his eyes. The bed was musty with stale hair oil. As he relaxed, sleep seized him triumphantly. For a second he struggled thinking, I'll dream about Frances, but when he fell asleep he did not dream at all.

CHAPTER THREE

He had met Frances for the first time at a fun-fair. He came out of the late evening gloom into the tungsten glare of coloured lights strung on poles and from booth to booth. Loudspeakers crashed out strident music that underlined the general clamour, the roar of the dodgems, the shrill screams of girls swung into mid-air on the ferris wheel. Under the red, green and blue bulbs the target guns snapped like sticks of dried wood and wooden balls thumped into the canvas barriers behind the coconut shy. A man in shirtsleeves yelled, 'Two cents a ball, six balls for ten,' at Beukes, but he shook his head and picked his way through the milling crowd, past the packed muddle in front of the ring pitchers and the line of women in front of the fortuneteller's booth. Sound pounded him and he rode with the blows, taking the rain of discordant voices, ecstatic cries from the whip and the embarrassed laughter on the merry-go-round mingled with the blaring roll of boogie-woogie. The recorded piano and brass shrieked like a storm at sea, all rhythm lost in the general roar of waves of ruptured decibels.

When Beukes had found that his friend Hamad was working overtime that night, he had turned towards the fair pitched in the suburban lot, having nothing else to do. He had three half-crowns and some pennies in his ticket pocket, and he wondered whether he should use them for throwing coconuts or pitching rings around the cheap vases, blonde dolls and bottles of eau-de-cologne which were carefully mounted and arranged so as to make it difficult to win any of them as a prize.

They've got everything organized to fox you, he thought, moving through the restless crowd. Dust rose from underfoot like brown smoke. He tripped over a rope and stumbled, and a dark face of badly-carved mahogany cried, 'Hey, man, hey, man, look what you doing, don't I say?' Then there were three others who manoeuvred skilfully to hedge him in against the side of a tent, and he saw the cynical smiles, stiff as frozen fish, and the cruel eyes, vulturine, under the peaks of padded caps.

'I say *mos*, pally,' one of them said. 'We need some ching *mos*, man.'

'Got none to spare,' Beukes said, his eyes alert for a chance to break out of the trap.

'He's a wise guy,' another said. 'I reckon he's a real wise burg, this.'

'Let's see what you got in your pockets, man,' the first one said. He had a grimy, pimply face like an unwashed, rusty vegetable grater. The music and the shouting crashed around them. A girl screamed on the dodgem cars.

The third one said, '*Ach*, leave him alone. Just another squashy, hair oil and all.'

'He's a wise guy,' the second one said. He looked the dangerous one, dangerous and septic as a rusty blade.

Beukes watched them all, his eyes shifting carefully from face to face, trying to predict which one would move first. Somebody nearby was shouting, 'I made it, I made it, man. The box of chocolates, that one with the horse on it.' Then somebody else was thrusting himself among them and a large man in overalls snapped: 'What's going on here then, hey? You *jubas* trying again to make nonsense, hey? Well, —— off, off this ground. I don't want to see you round here no more —— off.'

The gargoyle scowls were turned on the man in the overalls, they hesitated, shifting their feet like vultures disturbed at their prey, and they slowly turned and lurched off into the crowd.

The man in overalls said, 'I got my work cut out watching for buggers like them. Yesterday night somebody got robbed

35

and the law was here and the chief give me hell. Watch out, pally, old mate.'

'It's okay,' Beukes told him. 'I'll keep watch.' The man waved a hand not unlike a burnt ham and moved away, craning his neck over the heads of the jostling mass.

Beukes moved off into the crowd, aimlessly, still trying to decide whether to invest his money at the booths. Suddenly a voice cried out loudly, 'Hey, *ou* Buke, hey, what the hell you doing here, hey?'

He looked at the man who had shouted and smiled, 'Hullo, old Erny, howzit? Same thing you doing, I reckon.'

Erny cried, 'Long time no see. I lost fifteen bob on these games, man. It's a swindle. You reckon I'm a sucker? The only time you get your money's worth is on the swings and the big wheel and stuff like that. I took these goosies on the big wheel and they carried on like they was being murdered or something.'

Beukes looked at the two girls with Erny and said, 'Hullo there.' They smiled at him. One of them was holding a cut-glass bowl against her breast. She was a big girl with a hefty body, a heavy round face that showed that her upper front teeth were missing when she smiled. She also had dimples in her cheeks and that made her look charming in spite of the missing teeth and the heaviness.

'You win that?' Beukes asked, indicating the bowl.

'It was Erny,' she cried above the noise. 'He made a bullseye with the target shooting. Don't I say, Erny?'

'Listen, man, I'm a crack shot,' Erny yelled. 'Wil' Bill Hicock, hey.' He laughed. 'The *juba* at the stall didn't want to hand it over, the blerry crook, but I stood up for my rights, *mos.*'

'That's the ticket,' Beukes said. 'You all enjoying yourself?'

'We having a time,' Erny said.

'We're just wasting money,' the other girl put in. 'Erny shouldn't of brought us here, spending money on nonsense like that.'

'*Ach*, what the hell,' Erny cried. 'Eat, drink and be merry, that's what I say.' He laughed again and tried to slap this girl's behind, but she turned out of his reach, laughing.

Beukes looked at her. 'Erny always likes to throw his money around.'

'He could do a lot of other things with it,' the girl said and looked at Erny.

Around them the music blared interminably and the coloured lights on the ferris wheel went round and round through the illuminated uproar. The crowd milled and people pushed between them for a moment, separating them, the dust rose, and then they were together again. Beukes, looking at the girl once more as she waved a hand to clear the dust from her face, saw the smooth texture of her skin and the wide, slightly slanted eyes that were a strange colour in the glare of the fun-fair; he noticed the full, drawn bow of her mouth as she smiled and he thought, coffee and cream, she's all coffee and cream.

Then Erny was saying, 'Listen, what's the use standing around here? Let's go have more fun, man. Here I am with two goosies on my hands, so you better fall in, Buke.'

'Well, okay then,' Beukes said, glad to have company. 'What will we do? Roll pennies or throw rings?'

'Let's try for a box of chocolates, man,' the big girl said, looking in the direction of the coconut shy.

'Awright, awright,' Erny said, and to Beukes, 'By the way, mate, this is Mariam,' slapping the big girl playfully. 'She's a real bus, isn't she?'

'*Garn*,' the big girl cried. 'You always want to touch a person.'

'Ah, don't be like that,' Erny laughed. He grabbed the other girl's arm. 'This is Frances. She don't min' being touched.'

'You just try it,' the girl Frances, said laughing. 'You just try it, hey?'

'Well, let's go then,' Beukes said smiling at all of them.

37

'You reckon we should try throwing balls at coconuts?' Erny asked. He was a stout young man wearing a yellow Tee-shirt that clung to his torso. His arms were plump and hairy and he wore a gold watch and strap.

'I don't care,' Beukes said, feeling happy.

'It's wasting money,' Frances said.

But Mariam cried, 'Oh, man, Frances, don't be like that.'

'We're millernaires,' Erny said.

'You watch your money,' Beukes told him. 'There's some hard burgs around here. I got cornered by some of them.'

'Did they . . . ?' Frances started to ask.

'No, it was okay,' Beukes answered, pleased by her interest.

'We'll watch out,' Erny said. 'Not to worry. Well, come on, men.' He led the way and they pushed into the crowd.

'Don't get lost,' Beukes said to Frances. He was close behind her and he was not looking at anything around the fun-fair now, but at the crown of thick, soft black hair caught in her neck with a plastic clip.

Erny was shouting, 'Hell, with this crowd we never going to get to throw for that box of chocolates.' He was up ahead, his crew-cut head bobbing.

The dodgem cars thundered like a battlefield and voices shrieked with excitement while the wooden horses rose and fell with flaring, painted nostrils and ragged tails. A sign on a gaudy caravan said: *Madam Clair Will Read Your Future*.

'You want to have your fortune told?' Beukes asked Frances.

'Oh, I don't believe in that stuff,' she returned, smiling at him.

'Not even in the tall, dark stranger and the long journey?'

She shook her head, still smiling at him, and then looked about and cried, 'Where's Erny and Mariam? They're gone.'

Beukes scanned the jumbled faces about them. 'Hell, they're somewhere in the mob.' But there was no sign of them, and he asked her, 'Do you think we ought to look?'

'Where will we find them in this crowd?'

'Oh, hell.'

She said, 'Oh, I can look after myself.'

'I reckon you can. But you don't mind staying with me, hey?'

'That's okay.'

'Well, we could look for them at the coconut thing.'

'Oh, it's just a waste of time being here, anyway. I think I'll go home.'

'Don't go home yet, it's still early, man. Say, we can get out of this crowd, get something to drink. What do you say?'

'Awright, I am feeling thirsty; all this dust.'

He took her by an arm, saying, 'Don't get lost like the others.' Holding her arm and steering her ahead they picked their way through the shuffling mass that packed the fun-fair until they emerged through the fringe of the crowd, through a no-man's-land of empty soft-drink bottles, ice-cream cartons and potato-crisps packets. Beyond the pavement that fronted the fair the lights of the suburb made pale yellow splashes in the purple pool of the night.

'How, but I'm glad to be out of that,' Frances said. Her face shone in the orange glare of an electrolier and she sounded a little breathless.

'There's a place over there,' Beukes said and pointed towards a small oasis of red neon light that advertised a brand of soft drink. 'Do you think Erny and that girl will worry about you?'

'Why? I reckon they know we can find our own way.'

They crossed the trunk road, and walked side by side towards the cafe that stood in the shadow of a new flyover bridge. There were people strolling across the bridge and a fleet of cars swept along its curve like the moving glow of fairy lights.

There was nobody in the tiny cafe except for a woman with an Asiatic face under a green headkerchief. She had a row of bracelets on her arms and her eyelids were darkened with khol. A radio on a shelf was playing muted dance music. The woman with the Asiatic face didn't say anything, but stood behind the plastic-topped counter, waiting.

'What do you want?' Beukes asked the girl.

'Oh, anything. Make it pineapple.'

Beukes asked for two pineapple drinks and when they came he carried them, leading the way to one of the two small tables at the back of the shop. They sat down opposite each other under a sign that proclaimed the virtues of a stomach powder. The radio went on playing gently in the front of the shop, and from beyond the sound of the fun-fair drifted in.

'What made you visit the merry-go-round?' Frances asked as she sipped gassy pineapple soda through her straw.

'I was really on my way home from a bloke I know nearby,' Beukes said. 'I had nowhere else to go. He wasn't at home when I called. You like merry-go-rounds?'

'I just went with Erny and Mariam.'

'My aunty took me to a circus once when I was a lighty,' Beukes said. 'I didn't like it. The actors kept their backs to us all the time and you couldn't see anything they were doing. When I asked my aunty why, she told me it was because we were sitting in the segregated Coloured seats and the actors performed mostly for the Whites, even if we paid the same money. I never went to a circus again after that.' He drank some of his soda. Up front the radio throbbed quietly. 'You like dancing?' he asked. He had to find out about her, her likes and dislikes, prepare for every eventuality.

'Oh, I like dancing now and then,' Frances said. 'I went to a party last week, given by a netball club.'

'I'm no great dancer. I'm more of a listener, I reckon. Me and a pal, a bloke called Westy, we used to go to the City Hall some nights after evening school and listen to the municipal orchestra. I got to like some of the stuff they played.'

'My, you real highbrow.'

He laughed, 'I'm not, don't believe it.'

She said, 'I think I seen you before.'

'Yes? When?'

'You were helping at a meeting outside the place where I work.'

'You don't say. It's a small world, hey?'

He smiled and looking at her he saw that her slanting eyes were light brown in colour and very clear and bright. She wore no make-up of any sort and the skin of her unblemished face was smooth as amber silk. Under the sweep of black hair she wore small gold rings in her earlobes.

Beyond them the music stopped and a woman's voice announced the Mozambique station in Portuguese. Dance music started again; a car went past the cafe with the sound of escaping gas.

Frances asked, watching him, 'How did you get that mark under your eye?'

'Oh, this?' One hand raised a finger to it. 'I fell when I was a little boy still. We were playing cowboys in the street and I fell onto a tin can.'

'Shame.'

Looking at her he thought sentimentally that her face could be disfigured with a hammer and she would still look beautiful. Scars would not spoil her: instead they would give her face an added beauty.

'So you saw me before, hey?'

'Yes. You interested in political things?'

'I reckon so. Help out, now and then.'

'My pa goes to meetings and stuff like that.'

'What does he do?'

'Oh, he's a old-age pensioner. He gets seven pounds a month. My mummy the same.'

'So you're the breadwinner?'

'I reckon so. I got a married brother, but he don't live with us.'

A man came into the cafe and asked for cigarettes. He looked at the young man and the girl sitting there and then went out again when he had been served. The fun-fair rollicked in the distance. The woman with the khol-darkened eyes sat alone in the front of the shop under the fados from Portugal, the rows of bottled candies, and regiments of cigarettes.

Beukes was saying, 'I used to work in a factory too, once.

We made containers. You know, for jam and vegetables and things.'

'Oh. No, we make leather goods, belts, braces, handbags.'

'Your hands don't look like they work at a machine.'

'What do they look like then?'

'Like you do a lot of washing up.'

She laughed this time and Beukes looked again at the drawn bow of her mouth. He said: 'There was girls at our factory lost some of their fingers under the die-stampers.'

She winced, 'Oh, Lord.'

'Boss offered them jobs for life after that. Compensation and a job for life. They could work all their lives for five pounds a week.' He drank some more of the pineapple drink and remembered the hum and crash of the factory, the ranks of girls turning out thousands and thousands of bottle tops and box lids every day, hunched over the machines in their washed-out blue caps and smocks, moving like mechanical dolls.

'What you thinking about?' she asked, and he looked up at her and shook his head. 'Nothing. My mind was just wandering.'

She looked about, trying to find a clock. 'What's the time? I've got to get going.'

'Ah, stay, man,' he told her. 'I'll see you home. You live around here?'

'Not too far. I don't mind going home in the dark.'

'I'll see you home, don't worry.'

'Well, awright, if it's not too much trouble.'

He brought out a packet of cigarettes. 'Smoke?'

'Okay, I'll have one. I don't smoke very much, but all the girls in the faktry smoke.'

'I reckon so.'

She took a cigarette and held it to her mouth between two fingers and he struck a match and lighted it, looking at the curved length of her eyelashes. He lighted his own and she asked, with an eddy of blue smoke between them: 'You staying with your people?'

'My mother and father are both dead. They got killed in an accident when I was still a little boy.'

'I'm sorry,' she said and he saw the embarrassed look in her eyes.

'Oh, that was a long time ago. It was a Lodge picnic and the lorry went off the road.' He still entertained a vague memory of sitting at the edge of a ditch under trees, amid strewn suitcases, picnic baskets, clothes and scattered hard-boiled eggs, and voices were shouting, 'My God! my God! Allah! Allah! Allah!'

'Since then I lived with my uncle and aunty.'

'Oh.'

'They are okay. My aunty, Aunty Maudie I call her, used to be damn hot about the Union in her young days. I remember one day she came home – I was just out of school – she came home angry as a bugger and saying, "Those damn scabs. Here we are on strike and picketing the gates, and the blerry bitches tried to break through the line. But us girls," she said, "We gave them what for, awright." She showed me the broken heel of her shoe where she'd hit one of them with it. After that they gave her the sack, but she got a job in another factory. She was a good worker.'

Frances laughed and said, 'I reckon she must be a hard case.'

'Oh, she's very nice, man.'

The radio was now broadcasting news in Portuguese and the woman at the counter switched it off. A bus trundled past the cafe, windows bright in the navy-blue darkness. Frances said, 'We must be going. It is getting late.'

'Right-o, then,' Beukes said and got up. He helped her out of the chair and with his face coming near hers he could smell the perfume of her body, like scented soap, and saw the taut, high shapes of her full breasts under her blouse. Then they were going out of the cafe and he could feel the knot in his stomach as he walked behind her through the doorway.

In the big vacant space down the suburban road, the fun-fair

43

still assailed the night, its loudspeakers muted by distance, the strings of coloured lights glowing like signals behind a veil of dust. Beukes and the girl strolled along the road until she led him down a side street past rows of houses with dark gardens in front of them.

'You don't mind coming all this way, do you?' she asked.

'No, what. There's plenty of time for me to get the bus back.'

'Anyway, it is not too far. Do you live in town?'

'Yes. You been staying out here all the time?'

'Oh, yes. We been staying here ever since I was born. Not at the same place, though. Now we living in a council flat.'

They emerged into a lighted area with rows of shops closed for the night. Up the street a cinema was releasing a crowd of people; across its front sombrero-ed horsemen galloped, the hooves of the ponies raising yellow lithographed dust.

'You go to the flicks sometimes?' Beukes asked as they skirted the crowd that was splitting up, scattering for the bus stops.

'Now and then,' she said. 'Most of the time they show a lot of rubbish: cowboys and detectives and love stories that can't really happen.'

'Most girls like love stories and pictures.'

'I think it's because they hope it will happen to them – the way it happens on the screen, I mean.'

'You got a boy?'

She looked at him. 'No, not a special one.'

'What kind of boys do you fancy?'

'How do I know? I reckon I'll get married some day, but I don't know what kind of boy I'll get. Maybe somebody who'll beat me all the time.' She laughed and looked at him again in the half-dark because they were between street lights and then they were walking through a stretch that led towards big, rectangular blocks of flats which stood in rows, miles long, checkered with lighted windows.

'Anybody who'd want to slap you must be crackers,' he said.

44

'A few of my friends got married and the boys seemed real nice. But after they were married their husbands all turned out to drink too much and they fought with their wives all the time.'

'Oh, everybody's not the same,' Beukes said and now he wanted to take her hand, hold it all the way, but he felt suddenly awkward and nervous.

'No, I reckon not,' Frances said. 'This way.'

They crossed the road and came into the shadows of the great blocks, all alike, like barracks. 'I'm all right now,' Frances said. 'You don't have to come all the way.'

'Ah, I'll see you to your door,' Beukes told her. 'That's what a gentleman does, isn't it?'

'Oh, we are very polite,' she smiled. 'Okay then.'

In a courtyard with cracked flagstones and a worn-out patch of earth where grass had once grown, washlines made a network against the sky, looking deceptively like the steel wires high in a circus tent: one expected to see a group of aerialists, but instead, a set of overalls hung like a headless traitor on display. They crossed the courtyard to the entrance of the block.

Beukes said, 'Listen, can I see you again? Maybe we could go to a flick one night or maybe a hop or something.'

'Do you?'

'What?'

'Really want to see me again?'

'Why not?' he asked, and then boldly: 'You're a nice girl.'

'How do you know? We only just met.'

'Oh, I know, I know.'

'You're too sure, hey. And me, how do *I* know what kind of a chap you are?'

'Well, awright, if you don't want to . . .' He felt disappointed and a little angry, and also conscious of having given up too soon.

But she said, 'Oh, I didn't say I don't want to. I do go out with boys now and then.' She said it seriously, without cajolery.

'Right, then you'll see me again?'

Now she pretended to ponder and then finally beamed her smile at him in the light of the entrance way. 'Okay, when?'

'Make it Saturday.'

'Saturday? *Hmmm.*'

'Look,' he said. 'I'll come in the afternoon and we'll have all that time and then in the evening we could go somewhere, too.'

'My, you wanting a lot, hey? All my time, almost a whole day. Well, Saturday mornings I have to buy in the groceries and then in the afternoon I wash my hair . . .'

'Man, I'll come and look at you wash your hair. What do you say?'

'Well, if you don't mind sitting and talking to my pa while I get things straightened out in the flat . . .'

'Not at all, not at all. It's okay, then?'

'All right.'

They climbed two flights of concrete steps. Overhead a dull bulb glowed behind a thick plateglass panel, like a light in a prison, and on the walls a display of entwined hearts, lewd remarks, humorous verse and anatomical charts made crude murals in the municipal paintwork. Somewhere from behind a blank brown door a radio announced '. . . the Minister stated that increased expenditure . . .' while far away a car horned its way through the night.

She led the way along an outside balcony broken with standard brown doorways overlooking another courtyard with the inevitable washlines and cracked flagstones, and then stopped outside one of the doors. Beyond the balcony the rest of the estate stood barracked in the dark. Beukes looked at her and saw that now her face had become a little apprehensive, cautious, and he thought, smiling to himself, she thinks I'm going to try to kiss her. That's what they all think, I reckon.

46

Beyond her the stars were drawn together like wristlets of jewellery laid out on dusty velvet.

He turned to look back at the number on the door, to memorize it. She glanced at the number, holding her arms across her midriff, and said, 'Two-forty-four. Will you remember? And it's block D. You can get lost in this estate.'

'Don't worry, I'll remember.'

She felt that he was not going to take advantage, and looked up at him in the light on the balcony. He could see the white of her teeth between the slightly-parted lips, and the light-brown eyes as they surveyed him, trying to read his thoughts. Then he smiled at her and held out a hand, she looked at it and then took it and he could feel the coolness of her palm and the rough texture of worked fingers.

He said, 'Saturday then.'

'All right, I'll expect you.'

He released her hand and said good-night and then went along the balcony towards the landing. When he looked back she was not there. He had to run to catch the bus.

CHAPTER FOUR

The first thing Beukes saw when he woke up was the picture of the band leader smiling down at him in the room. From beyond the curtain behind the ewer and jug, early twilight smudged the street with gentian fingers. The picture smiled down like an ikon, as if Tommy had substituted the worship of dance-music for religion. The radiogram stood like an altar in the gloom and the wafers of stacked records waited for communion with the faithful. He'll never grow up, Beukes thought; the bloody clown's mental development must have stopped in his teens.

But Tommy was a good friend. Beukes trusted him with simple courier tasks and he had managed them without a hitch. You had to make do with the material you found at hand. Nowadays you could hardly pick and choose; you could not be too fussy. It was like a bride unable to afford the expensive gown seen in a glossy magazine: she had to make do with a copy. The movement writhed under the terror, bleeding. It had not been defeated, but it had been beaten down. It crouched like a slugged boxer, shaking his spinning head to clear it, while he took the count, waiting to rise before the final ten. Life still throbbed in its aching arms and fingers; wholesale arrests had battered it. The leaders and the cadres filled the prisons or retreated into exile. Behind them, all over the country, tiny groups and individuals who had escaped the net still moved like moles underground, trying to link up in the darkness of lost communications, and broken contacts. Some of them knew each other and wrestled to patch up the body. They trusted each other because without trust they were useless. They burrowed underground, changing their nests and their lairs frequently. Those who were known to the police

walked in fear, shaken, hoping that they might be able to disappear before the police decided that their time had come.
Little by little the raw nerve fibres and tired muscles of the
movement established shaky communication with centres
aboard.

But it's as shaky as hell, Beukes thought. It's like shivering
in the cold. But you hung on, sometimes because you understood why, often because there was nothing else to do. You
couldn't say, the hell with it, I'm going home. So you sat tight
and did what you had to do, hoping for the best, depending
here and there on crazy buggers like Tommy. Thank God
they weren't all like Tommy, mostly undependable, risky. Hell,
Tommy was all right, as long as you told him exactly what to do.
There were very good people in the movement and the fact that
they still operated bucked you up when you started feeling that
it was all useless. They were like asprin for fatigue or a bad
headache.

Lying in the gloom of the late summer evening that spread
across the walls and clogged the corners with shadows, he
tried to think of Francy, but he could not conjure her up,
because he was worrying about Tommy and whether he would
make a balls-up of a simple courier job. Somewhere in the
slummy street somebody yelled and a distant cry answered
back across the cracked paving, the broken asphalt, the tired
scraps of paper in the gutters. After a while sleep touched him
again and he nodded at it, slack-mouthed.

He was on the ferris wheel at the fun-fair, being lifted
upwards and then lowered again into pale orange light. The
wheel went round and round vertically and he rose and fell
with the motion. The light teased his eyes, and then somebody
was tugging him from side to side while he swung up and down
so that he lurched limply, unable to resist, like a rag doll in the
jaws of a terrier. Then he was waking up and the light was on
his eyeballs through the eyelids. His eyes opened slowly,
heavily, like the rising portcullis of a castle, and there was
Tommy grinning down at him, holding him by a shoulder.

Beukes stared at him for a while and Tommy said: 'You had a good sleep, *ou* Buke? I got something for you here, man.'

'Ah, it's you,' Beukes said. He hoisted himself up on one elbow and yawned into the other fist. His body was moist with perspiration. The light in the room was on now but the window was still open to let a faint breeze stir the curtain. Beukes sat up and swung his feet onto the floor, resting his elbows on his knees.

Tommy straightened up and said: 'There's a letter and that parcel there.' On the table was a bundle wrapped in greasy newspaper. It steamed gently.

'What's that?' Beukes asked frowning and looking up at Tommy. He was still sleepy and his mind functioned sluggishly.

Tommy said, 'Oh, not that parcel. That's some fish and chips I bought for us. This is the one.' And he indicated a flat, rectangular package wrapped and gummed in brown paper, which lay beside the bundle of fish and chips. 'Here's your letter, pal.' Tommy held up a white envelope.

Beukes yawned and took the envelope. It was of the ordinary kind, sold at any stationer's, and the flap had been gummed down and then sealed with a torn-off patch of gum paper. Beukes looked at the envelope. There was nothing written on the front. He examined the brown seal. That doesn't mean anything, he thought; anybody could have read what's inside, put it back in another envelope and pasted a piece of gum paper over the flap – Polsky, Tommy, anybody. It's a gamble, he thought. You did this work, taking a chance all the time, hoping the bugger behind you or the one ahead of you would play the game.

Tommy was saying, 'You mus' be hungry. We'll have the fish and chips now and I'll make some coffee. Find it a bother to boil tea. Tea for two, hey? You feel like a drink, Buke? I got half a bottle of sherry somewhere.'

'No,' Beukes said. 'Thanks. I'll only get sleepy again, drinking wine.'

Tommy was taking down plates from a shelf and setting them

out on the table. He rummaged in a drawer and found knives and forks. They did not match and one of the forks had a bent prong. He grinned as he straightened the prong and asked, 'Love letter?'

'Like hell,' Beukes said. Sleep had dropped from him like a shed blanket. He sat on the edge of the bed and tore off one end of the envelope, holding it up to the light first. Tommy was humming a tune while he set out salt and pepper and a bottle of tomato sauce that was thickly clogged around the neck with what looked like coagulated blood.

Tommy sang softly, 'I'm always chasing rainbows . . .' while Beukes drew the paper from the envelope. He unfolded the message and looked at it. It was a carbon copy, but there was an addition in original typewriting below. Tommy was unwrapping the fish and chips, placing a slab of fish on each plate and dividing the fried potatoes.

Beukes read the carboned message: 'Leaflets herewith. Leaflets must be distributed in your section on the night of Thursday (there was a date) but not before or after. Repeat, only Thursday night. Those responsible for distribution are reminded to take all necessary precautions.'

All necessary precautions, Beukes thought with a touch of sourness. I should bloody well think so. Some of those passing out the handbills would probably have the jitters all the time they did it. Perhaps one or two would dump their allocations in the nearest sewer and sneak off home with their hearts in their mouths and a sense of relief. But he knew that most of the handbills would go out, their handlers slipping from door to door in the dark, hearts hammering with fear or minds cold with courage, sneaking the rectangles of paper into letterboxes, under doors, dropping them onto garden paths or snapping them under the windscreen-wipers of parked cars. In the morning a lot of the tracts would be in the hands of the political police *and then the hunt would be up again.*

Tommy announced, 'Supper's ready, Buke, *ou* pal. Better eat now or it will be cold.'

51

Beukes was reading the extra part of the message. It would be meant for him only, and perhaps one or two others. 'Three recruits north. Contact Hazel Friday.'

Tommy asked, 'Ready, Buke?'

'Okay,' Beukes said, getting to his feet. He pulled on his trousers, thinking, hope Friday's not too soon after the distribution. The bloody place will be crawling with cops, man. I hope they bladdy know what they're doing. He thrust the message and envelope into a trouser pocket and stood stretching the residue of sleep out of his body. His mind was nervous and there was a cold feeling in his stomach. You're worrying again; you're worrying because you're never sure that everybody will do his part. You give them instructions and then leave them and then you sweat, wondering whether they'll do the ——ing job properly. *And on Friday morning the hunt will be up for them.* All the suspects on the police lists would be raided, questioned. Some of them might be taken away. They would disappear for God knew how long; the political police no longer needed to give any account. Yes, the hunt would be up.

Tommy said, 'I must go to a committee meeting tonight. Our ballroom club, you know *mos*. That awright with you, *ou* Buke?'

Beukes drew up a chair and sat down at the table. He said, picking up his knife and fork, 'Yes, man, but I've got to go out, too.' He speared a portion of fish. 'I'll be away all night, I reckon.'

Tommy splashed his fish with tomato sauce and looked at Beukes interestedly. 'All night?'

'I have to do some things,' Beukes told him. 'It'll take all night, maybe.'

'That's nice, that's nice, man.' Tommy grinned and his teeth lit up like lamps in the darkness of his face. He hummed *My Blue Heaven* while he worked at the crackling slab of fish with his fork.

Beukes asked, looking at him curiously, 'What the hell, you bloody well sing when you eating, too?'

Tommy said, 'Youse too serious, *ou* Buke, too serious like. Me, I take things *mos* easy all the time.' He filled his mouth with fish and potato and chewed.

'Too bladdy easy,' Beukes said. 'Too bladdy easy. There's people worrying their brains out in this world and you just take it easy.'

'Ah, why worry? If you worry you die, if you don't worry you also die,' Tommy said. 'This fish is blerry stale.' He picked a fishbone from his mouth. 'You can't depen' on nobody. Lookit this stale fish, hey? I ask for fresh stockfish. This must have come out of the blerry Ark.'

'Bit of snook wouldn't of been bad,' Beukes said. 'I haven't tasted snook for a long time.'

'It isn't *mos* the season for snook,' Tommy said. He was glad the subject had changed. Not only did he avoid any serious kind of discussion, but was incapable of fathoming the things Beukes often talked about. For Tommy reality, life, could be shut out by the blare of dance-bands and the voices of crooners. From this cocoon he emerged only to find the means of subsistence, food and drink. Politics meant nothing to him. He found it easier to live under the regime than to oppose it.

Now he said, 'We got our committee meeting tonight. We want to run a ballroom dancing competition.'

Beukes said, shaking his head, 'Ballroom competition.' Then, 'Listen, I've got to have something to carry this stuff in.' He indicated the parcel on the table, lying among the plates, the bottle of sauce and the chipped cups. 'You got a kind of bag for me or something?'

Tommy looked at the parcel and said, 'Hmmm. Well, there's the satchel I keep our minutes and stuff in, but it'll be too small. Anyway, I need it tonight for the meeting.' He thought for a moment while Beukes went on eating, then looked around the room and said, 'Hey, you can use the record case. It'll do, won't it?'

He left his chair and bounced over towards the wardrobe. He opened the door and rummaged inside, throwing out crumpled clothes, soiled shirts, worn socks, and finally produced a dusty brown cardboard case of the kind gramophone records are carried in. It was narrow and rectangular, with the locks and handle in the narrow end.

'There. Will that do?'

'Looks okay,' Beukes replied. 'Thanks, Tom.'

'Not to mention.' Tommy brought the case over and put it on the floor by the table. He sat down again to finish his meal. Beukes wiped his plate clean with a potato chip and popped it into his mouth. 'I'll most probably be back early in the morning. Before you go to work.'

'You a blerry owl,' Tommy said grinning. 'A blerry owl fiddling around in the night. Nights is for fun, not work.'

'You right,' Beukes told him. 'You damn well right. Man ought to have fun at night.'

'That's *mos* what I say.'

Tommy got up and went to plug in the electric kettle on the cupboard. Coming back he said, 'Meeting suppose to start at eight, but we always really get together at the bar nearby first for some drinks.'

Beukes asked, 'What in hell you talk about at a meeting like that?'

'Minutes and things,' Tommy said, gathering up the used plates and dumping them in an enamel basin he had taken from the cupboard. 'Matters arising. We want to run a party for funds, too. End of the year we going to have a picnic.'

Beukes said, 'Christ,' and got out his cigarettes. He lighted one and looked at his watch. 'Twenty-five past seven.'

'It's not very dark yet,' Tommy said. 'Get's dark late this time of year.'

Beukes got to his feet and went around the table to the window behind the washstand. He parted the curtain a little and peered out. He saw only the disused balcony with its splintered boards and the old wrought-iron rails and part of the building opposite. He could not see the street.

54

Tommy asked, taking a jar of instant coffee from the wardrobe, 'What you looking for, Buke?'

'Did you see anybody hanging about downstairs when you came home? Strangers?'

Tommy looked at him with puzzled eyes. 'Strangers? I dunno. I reckon there's always strangers hanging about like. People you don' know. What's the matter?'

'Nothing,' Beukes told him. 'It's nothing.'

Tommy sounded anxious. 'Hey, you don't reckon ...'

'It's nothing, man.'

Tommy stood there holding the jar of coffee. 'I hope nothing's wrong, hey.'

'It's nothing, man,' Beukes said again. 'If they was suspicious they'd be up here awready.'

'They?'

Then Beukes smiled at him with the long upper-lip, feeling suddenly wicked. 'Who do you think?' He drew a finger across his throat and made a tearing sound with his mouth, still smiling. Then he said, 'Forget it. You just stick to your ballroom, chum.'

Tommy spooned coffee into the cracked cups on the table and said, looking anxious, 'Ou Buke, I don't *mos* mind doing stuff and things for you now and then, but I don't want to get into no trouble, hey. I mean likely, I do it because you an ol' pal of mine, not for politics and stuff.'

Beukes said, blowing smoke from his nostrils, 'Oh, don't take on, man. You in no trouble. Uncle Buke will see to that.'

Tommy smiled again. 'Okay, Buke, I take your word for it. Well, I made the coffee.'

Beukes sat down again and drew up one of the cups. Somebody went down the hallway, heavy footsteps thumping on the bare floorboards, and for a moment his heart constricted and he felt his scalp crawl. But the footsteps died away, a door slammed somewhere and there was silence again beyond the room. He thought, there isn't any safe hideaway, you can't relax any-bloody-where; just live with your ears cocked, that's all.

Tommy said, 'Must I put on a record?' He had been too long from the shrine, the massed choirs of brass and reeds.

Beukes blew steam from his coffee and asked, 'What sort of discs you got? All that ballroom stuff?'

'You can't get decent records nowadays, man. All they sell is that yeah-yeah-yeah. The old style is gone.'

'You can say that again,' Beukes said, sipping his coffee. 'The old style is gone in a lot of ways.' He remembered the rallies, the blaring loudspeakers, the banners sagging between their poles, the applause. Sometimes we even had a band. The thought of bands brought him back to Tommy. Youth nudged him with a nostalgic elbow, and he asked: 'You got any really good jazz?'

'I've got some old Ambrose,' Tommy answered, looking hopeful.

'Not that, man,' Beukes laughed. Then seriously, 'You ever hear Dorsey playing Rimsky-Korsakov's *Song of India*?'

'What's that?'

'You wouldn't know,' Beukes said. 'Ziggy on trumpet.' In his mind's ear he heard again the riding Elman trumpet pealing through the reeds. 'That's from a long time ago.'

'I remember from years back, Buke, you *mos* use to like that kind of stuff. Glen Miller.'

'He was too sugary.'

'Well, I like ol' Louis. Everyborry like ol' Louis, hey.' Tommy started to hum *Blueberry Hill*, rolling his eyes and trying to sound gravel-throated.

Beukes laughed, watching him. He thought, hell, when did I last feel like this? Youth and happiness lasted a while, like the taste of candy in the mouth of a hungry child. He laughed, 'You'll never sound like Louis.'

'I saw Mario Lanza in a film long ago.'

'That boy? Go on, he couldn't sing. Most of the time he was just screaming his head off, man.'

'They said he sang like Caruso.'

'Caruso, crack. There were far better tenors. Tito Gobbi and so on.'

'I don't go for that classical stuff.'

Beukes swallowed some coffee: 'You ever hear Schwartzkopf or Victoria De Los Angeles?'

'Who's they?'

'What's the use,' Beukes said. He looked at Tommy. 'There's things poor people just don't get a chance to learn or hear.' He looked at his wrist-watch. 'Well, it's nearly eight.'

'Oh God, I got to go.' Tommy leapt up from the table. 'The committee will be waiting at the Royal Arms.' He sounded as anxious as a Minister late for a Cabinet meeting and said hurriedly, 'Here we been talking . . .' and went quickly to the wardrobe, bundling the strewn clothing back into it. He turned again, holding a shabby leather satchel and a jacket of small check material. He dropped the satchel on the floor and struggled into the jacket. 'I hope you don' min' me going off like this, Buke.' He could not resist humming, 'Putting on my top-hat, putting on my white tie, putting on my tails.'

'You go ahead,' Beukes said, near to laughter. 'You look like the world would come to an end if you miss the first drink.'

Tommy picked up his satchel again and went to the door. He paused with his hand on the knob, standing there worriedly in the black dress trousers and checked jacket, and said: 'Oh, yes, if you go, leave the key on top of the door frame, hey?'

'Will it be safe there?'

'Sure man, it will be okay. Only let nobody see you do it.' He opened the door. 'Goo' night, Buke. Be seeing you, hey.' And added musically, 'In all the old familiar places.'

When Tommy was gone, Beukes went over to the table and sat down again. He drew the brown paper parcel, which Tommy had brought, towards him and tore away the gummed strips which sealed it, ripping off the wrapping. There were stacks of small, printed handbills, each stack bound with a strip of gum paper. Beukes picked up one of the packets and riffled the end of it with a thumb. Like a bladdy bank robber counting the loot, he thought, sitting there under the pale, bare electric light in the shabby room. Somewhere in the building water pipes gurgled and a door banged. Footsteps stuttered downstairs.

Beukes pulled one of the handbills from a pile and looked at it. It was printed in small type with black headlines here and there. It was a neat printing job, unlike the hand-rolled kind they had turned out in the back rooms of suburban houses. He remembered the job they had done in the store-room behind the butcher's shop, among the dangling meat cleavers and salami sausage, with the sawdust underfoot and the mincing machine that had got in the way. We're making progress, he thought wryly. He wondered where the leaflets had been printed; who had brought them in; had they been transported in parcels like this in crates, or in cabin-trunks with false bottoms? Or maybe we've set up a whole printing plant somewhere here at home. No, that would be too risky; the stuff must come from outside, arranged by some exiled committee or other. He didn't know. The less you knew, the better.

He read the handbill. 'We bring a message ... you will wonder that men and women would risk long terms of imprisonment to bring you this message. What kind of people do these things? The answer is simple. They are ordinary people who want freedom in this country ... From underground we launched the new fighting corps ... sent youth abroad to train as people's soldiers, technicians, administrators ... We will fight back ... To men who are oppressed freedom means many things ... Give us back our country to rule for ourselves as we choose ... Many ways to fight for freedom ...'

When he had read the handbill through he could feel the prickling in his scalp, down his back. *By the week-end they would be searching for them.* He put the paper down and rubbed the palms of his hands along his thighs. Then he thought angrily, the sons of bitches, we aren't dead yet, not by a bladdy long chalk.

He picked up the record case Tommy had given him and shook it out. A little dust drifted down, but otherwise it was empty. Thrusting packets of handbills into the case, Beukes thought, well, it serves for something else besides foxtrots and quicksteps; the packets of handbills fitted neatly into the case. Beukes shut the lid and snapped the locks. He knew the names and addresses of those to whom he would deliver the leaflets. He did not have any information written down anywhere. He kept that in his head; he wasn't one of those little-black-book agents they showed in the movies.

It was a little cooler in the room now that evening was closing in. He got up and took off his clothes and then went over to the wash-table by the window. He poured cold water into the basin and then found a wash-rag that looked and felt like cold grey tripe. He sponged himself all over with it and one of Tommy's soiled towels dried him. When he had dressed again his shirt and singlet still felt a little warm with perspiration, but his body felt cool. He knotted his necktie, looking at himself in the wardrobe mirror: the copper-brown eyes and the long upper-lip grinned alertly. They still have to catch this fox, he thought. As he pulled on his coat, his mind sang: *A-hunting we will go, we'll catch a fox and put him in a box, a-hunting we will go.* Feeling in his trouser's pocket he found the message which had come with the parcel. Contact Hazel Friday. He produced cigarettes and matches and lighted one, then held the match to the message and watched the paper turn brown, then lick into flame and disintegrate into the ashtray below it.

He picked up the record case and looked about. He put the case down again and went over to the bed, straightened the bedclothes and then went back to pick up the case. His parcel containing the shaving kit and pyjamas was still beside the wash-basin, but he left it, knowing he meant to be back. He went over to the door and opened it, turned off the light and took the key. Outside in the narrow hallway there was nobody about. Beukes shut the door and locked it. Nobody came out

59

of the rooms along the hallway. He placed the key on the ledge above the door and went down the hallway carrying the case. Halfway down the hall he remembered that he had not emptied the wash-basin, but he did not turn back. The staircase was dim and somewhere downstairs a man was singing, otherwise the house was silent. Beukes went downstairs and the steps creaked all the way to the entrance.

CHAPTER FIVE

The blue evening fell like a curtain over the last act of the day. The air outside was cool and approaching autumn touched the weather with a warning finger from afar. The lamps had not come on yet and along the street people sat in dim doorways or on verandahs, drab phantoms and tawdry spectres of saints among the ruins of abandoned cathedrals, like characters in some obscurely metaphysical play. A cigarette glowed here and there against the background of murmured gossip and sporadic laughter like noises heard in the wings.

Beukes stood for a moment on the sidewalk outside the house and watched the street. Where the evicted old woman had sat amid her belongings, there was only an empty cardboard box toppled into the gutter. Satisfied that there was nothing unusual about the surroundings, he walked down the street, taking his time, casually carrying the case stuffed full of handbills. Endangered life was crowded between walls of cheap cardboard: the penalty for urging the armed overthrow of the goverment could be death. But with his everyday brown suit, the anonymous hang of the shoulders, he was just somebody going somewhere.

He crossed a section that had the look of an area cleared after a bombing. The district would be developed for White 'middle-class occupation' the newspapers had said. He made his way towards the main road to the suburbs having decided to deliver the handbills far out first and work his way back.

In a darkening street a brace of bandits in the guise of two small boys with torn clothing and snotty faces emerged from an alleyway and levelled their wooden pistols at him. 'Hey, mister, give us a cent, man. Give a cent, mate.' He grinned at them and went by, defying the ambush, and they yelled after him, 'Hey, hey there, you ape.' They followed him a little way, firing their pistols at him, and then gave up the chase.

On the main road he bought a late evening newspaper from a youth with the face of a young wolf and a set of overalls three sizes too large. Then he made his way past closed wholesalers and abandoned market stalls towards a bus-stop. The ruins of a once well-patronized cinema stood across the way like the leftovers of an earthquake. A stained and torn poster on a sagging board ironically advertised an old film: *Hurricane*. To the west the tops of the city were silhouetted like cut-outs against the aurora of neon signs.

The local street lights came on and he stood at the bus stop with watchful brown eyes, a brown man in a brown suit, carrying a flat cardboard case and a newspaper folded under an arm. A suburban trolleybus approached and he waved at it, climbed to the Coloured upper-deck and found a seat at the back. He placed the case on his lap and got out a cigarette, looking casually at the passengers in front of him. The upper-deck was half-full. There was nobody there that looked like a police agent; but then what did one look like?

Beukes opened the newspaper and began to read. The day's proceedings in the trial of the murderess took up most of the front page: 'It was during the summer that she decided to kill her husband. She began to add a little bit of the white powder which contained arsenic to his coffee. Since he took milk, she would put the deadly white powder in the cup first and then pour in the steaming coffee.' In a side column the Minister of Police announced: 'The Republic is facing a new wave of guerilla incursions on its northern borders . . . African nationalist infiltrators are stirring up the local population.' He read on, intermittently looking up to check the bus-stops, until it was time to get off. Depositing the newspaper in a trash-can, he walked past a row of shut but lighted shops and then turned down a sloping street between semi-detached houses towards a small square that fronted the entrance to the suburban railway station.

The Non-White ticket office was lighted and a short queue of travellers were buying tickets at the tiny window. The ticket machine went jolt-jolt and beyond the door to the platform the signals clacked and creaked. Beukes did not buy a ticket because he was merely using the station as a short-cut. He went past the line of travellers and onto the platform. There were a few people waiting for the train to the city. It was just past the time when people had ceased work for the day and the trains from the city would be carrying the biggest crowds. This station was the stop for the bus route to the Coloured and African settlements, and Beukes stood on the platform waiting for the next train in from the city so that he could join the crowd. He strolled towards the entrance to the subway for Non-Whites to cross to the other side of the station. Beyond the station was the bus terminus with big yellow buses trundling to and from the shelters where the queues waited.

Then he saw something else. At the exit of the subway, on the other side of the station, a police barrier had been erected. Lamp-light fell on uniforms and flat caps, the blue tops and lighter blue trousers of the civil police; and by parked Volkswagens and Fords, plain clothes men with clay faces smoked blurred cigarettes. Above them on a huge billboard a happy family drank Coca Cola, smiling down with merry faces.

Beukes cursed under his breath. In a clearing stood two big police trucks and already there were people crowded behind the wire mesh of one of them: shabby bundles of secondhand clothes ready for transport to a sale. They would have been found without the necessary permits to live in the area, or, in some cases, in possession of dope or for being drunk, or for numerous other offences. This was known as a 'routine check' because the police were concentrated only on the exit from the subway. Beukes turned immediately and made his way back. His heart beat a little pronouncedly. People who were not White – even the criminally innocent – always reacted that way. There were a hundred and one crimes one might have committed without knowledge. Palpitations of the heart had become a national disease.

He left the station by a side entrance and was back in the square. He would have to use the motorbridge across the railway lines. There were footbridges across the station, of course, but there was no point in using them. He dared not risk using the White footbridge which gave access to another part of the district: a Coloured man had recently been sentenced to twenty pounds or ten days for taking a short cut across a White bridge. Sterner measures would be taken if the practice continued, the magistrate had said.

The motorbridge overlooked the shining junction of rails and overhead powerlines, the Coca Cola billboard, the bus terminus and the police block. Looking through the girders as he moved along the footpath that flanked the carriageway, he could see the waiting police, the skeletal metal outline of a slung sten-gun, the gleam of brass of a belt buckle.

Down near the subway where the police trucks stood, the constable with the sten-gun was saying: 'Thank the Lord that I am off on Saturday. The season starts and I want to see the first match.' He was young and burly and had a pale, chubby face blemished by small pimples.

'Who plays?' asked his mate who leaned against the fender of one of the trucks, his thumbs in his pistol belt.

'Wellington against Somerset West,' the one with the sten-gun and the pimples replied.

'*Ach*, it is not such a wonderful start of the season,' the other told him derisively. 'Wellington and Somerset West. They are but two weak teams. For rugby there is nothing like Villagers.'

'Are you off Saturday?'

'No, man.'

The one with the sten-gun laughed. 'Then you are just jealous, *mos*. I reckon you would enjoy being on the field, whether they are weak teams or no.'

'Man, I can *mos* go the following week. In any case, it will

64

be station duty only. It is not so bad on station duty over the week-end.'

The policeman with the pimples eased the strap of his sten-gun and said, '*Ja,* it is better than to stand about in the night like this, or walking a beat.'

'Don't you like the force?'

'*Ach,* it's awright.'

'You could buy yourself out.'

'For what reason? It is okay, man. The pay is okay, you get off duty.'

'*Ja,* to watch the rugby match.'

'And to see my girl.' The chubby face grinned in the lamp-light.

The second policeman laughed. 'So you have a girl, huh? A boy like you.'

The one with the sten-gun chuckled and said boastfully: 'Do not concern yourself, man. I am not so much of a boy as you think.'

'How is the girl then?'

'Not bad, not too bad. I'll see her after the match.'

'What will you do?' The second man spoke slyly, grinning at the pimply one. 'What the blerry hell can you do with a girl?'

'Don't worry, I know how to handle one.'

'Like *ou* Gesper?'

The policeman with the sten-gun looked serious and said, 'That is not a thing to joke about.'

'Jesus, to do a thing like that over a woman.'

'That thing can get under one's skin.'

'You go to hell,' the one who was leaning against the truck said. 'As long as I can get it when I want it I don't give a *donder* who it comes from. Why, in the station even, it is easy. They bring in drunk women, even hottentots.'

'Not that kind, I wouldn't touch that kind.'

'It's all the same. Do you reckon I'm crazy to go and strangle a girl and then shoot my head in just because one girl won't part with it? I must be *bedondered,* crazy.'

'It wasn't because of that,' the burly young policeman said. 'Old Gesper was in love with her and she would not have him.'

'So there are others with the same meat, man.'

'Man, you do not understand.'

The other policeman laughed. '*Jong*, I only understand one thing, that thing. But you are a *slim kerel*, a wise guy. Lot of knowledge about such matters.'

'Anyway, it was a sad thing. We were all very upset at the station. The commandant made a speech and everybody contributed to the collection for a wreath.'

'For the girl, or for Gesper?'

The chubby-faced policeman shook his head and said, 'Man, you talk bad luck.'

The other policeman threw back his head and laughed again, and it sounded like the whinnying of a pony. He straightened up and walked in a small circle, looking at the shiny toecaps of his regulation shoes, smiling. In the distance the siren of a train whooped and the powerlines above the permanent way quivered. A sergeant broke away from a group of police and came over towards them.

'Van Graan,' he said to the one who had been leaning against the truck. 'Go you to the other side, the other side of the station there, and send all the kaffirs this way.'

'Right, sergeant.' The policeman clicked his heels and then marched off into the subway. The one with the chubby face and the sten-gun followed the sergeant and took up his position by the barricade.

Crossing the motorbridge, Beukes saw the train pull into the station and the next moment the platform was crowded with passengers streaming towards the subway. Around the police block the stream swirled against the dam of blue uniforms and the jerking flashlights, then slowly trickled through accompanied by shouts and curses. Lunchboxes, bundles, bags were being searched, papers examined.

'I say, sarge I'm in a hurry, let me through.'

66

'F—— you. Who in the blerry hell do you think you are? Let me see what you got in that parcel.'

'Just my overalls, *meneer*, just my overalls. Taking them home to be washed.'

'Open up, you hell, before I *donder* you.'

'Hey, what the hell goes on there in front? A man must *mos* get home for supper.'

'Jesus, working all day and now there is this hold up.'

'*Jong, waar's jou pas?* Where's your pass?'

Pale white fingers like maggots flicked over the pages, identifying the bearer against the photograph. 'Lord, all you *bliksems* look the blerry same. Where did your mother get you from, hey?' The pages rustled one over the other. 'Hey, hey, you did not pay your tax this year, hey?'

'I paid the poll tax months ago.'

'Like blerry hell you did. Come along, boy, come along.'

'I paid.'

'F—— you. You think I'm a bloody baboon? And don't give me your bloody cheek either. Here, constable, take this one to the van.'

'But if you look you will see the stamp.'

'Listen to me, *bliksem,* do you think I have got time to waste? Think you I have got all night to listen to you? You can tell it all to the magistrate *bass.*'

'*Jong*, come along, jump, jump.'

'Jong, kom, kom, kom, pas, man, pas.'

'What the f——ing hell you got in that pocket. *Dagga*, hey? You bastards live on that f——ing weed, I reckon.'

'It's only my tobacco.'

'*Jong*, let me see. Shake out those pockets.'

'F—— the law.'

'Who said that? You bastards there at the back, I'll get you. Stop that *verdomde* pushing there.'

'Listen, you baboon, this pass book is no good, you should have been out of this city a long time ago already. You reckon you can cheat the government, hey?'

67

'But I am working here, sir.'

'Oh, yes? And who gave you permission to work in this city? It is trouble for you, you black baboon. Here's another one, sergeant.'

'Into that van, jump, jump, jump, man.'

Reaching the end of the bridge, Beukes saw a group of men being thrust towards the truck, covered by a young policeman with a sten-gun. From the bus shelters the queues of waiting people watched bleakly. The big yellow buses came in and out of the terminus, swaying heavily as they edged across the broken concrete. Those released by the police block were dodging the buses to get into the queues.

Beukes left the bridge and crossed the road, walking a short distance towards a corner where he knew the buses would turn on their way out. He was out of sight of the station and he was sure the police were not going to leave the barricade to search beyond it. Nevertheless, he waited with anxiety worrying at his stomach like a trapped animal trying to escape a pitfall. A bus swung carefully around the corner, but it was not the one he wanted, and he waited for the next one while anxiety turned to anger and then back to the scratching worry.

When his bus turned the corner, slowing down, he stepped off the kerb and swung clumsily onto the packed platform. A hand grabbed him and a voice cried, 'Hold on, mate.' He nodded his thanks and squeezed into the jam.

The passengers overflowed onto the platform and crowded on the stairs to the upper-deck. On the platform a tipsy man with a red-eyed face stained with coal dust was arguing with somebody near him, complaining that the bunch of fish which he had brought home from the harbour was being squashed. 'Well, I can't help it then, can I?' the other passenger told him.

'Look, pally, this fish cos' me five bob. By the time you finish with it, is going to be soft as crack, don't I say?'

'Then you should *mos* have taken another bus, pally. I can't help it.'

'They ought to get more buses,' somebody said.

'More buses?' a woman put in. 'You reckon they going to bother about our comfort? Company just colleck the money and the hell with you.'

The conductor struggled down the staircase calling, 'Fares, please, your fares ready, please.'

'Hey you, *ou* guard-*tjie*,' a man called. 'When you going to get extra buses on this run then? A man *mos* pay his fare to ride in comfort, don't I say?'

The conductor, who was harrassed and irritable, snapped, 'Write to the bloody company, don't ask me.'

'Oh, he's a clever then, that one.'

'Fares, please. All fares.'

'I say, *ou* guard-*tjie*, how you going to colleck the fares on this f——ing bus? You might as well let everybody ride for nothing, I reckon.'

'Ride for nothing? It's *mos* my job to colleck fares, man. The company pay me to do my job.'

'Ah, so youse a boss-boy, hey?' The crowd on the platform laughed.

'Okay, I's a boss-boy, so what.'

'A fuggen arse creeper, that's what.'

'Let a man get through here, please.'

'F—— the company, f—— the bosses. They just making f——ing money out of us poor people.'

'Here,' a woman cried angrily. 'Haven't you got no manners to swear like that. Didn't your old ones bring you up proper?'

'Awright, missus, I ask excuse. But if it isn't one thing, is something else, reckon and think. On the train is the blerry law and now on the bus is this basket.'

The conductor looked angry and said: 'Don't you talk to me so, hey? I'm not your play-mate.'

'*Gwan*, who want you for a play-mate then? *Gwan*.'

'I will put you off the bus, hear me?'

'You know what you can do with your blerry bus?'

'Quiet, quiet,' the woman cried. 'Behave yourself. A decent person can't ride on the bus no more.'

'Aaah, maybe missus ought to ride on the European bus then.'

'Don't be cheeky with me. You don't know how to talk to older people.'

The bus conductor had squeezed his way inside and was calling again for fares. Every hundred yards or so the bus slowed down at a stop but nobody alighted or climbed aboard on this long stretch of road. They passed the municipal stables with the dust-cart horses grazing in a small patch of grass.

Another man said, 'Those law grabbed old Ali.'

'What for then?'

'I dunno. They was shaking his pockets and before you know then they *mos* escort him to the wagon. The f——ing government just making money out of fines, you know them.'

'They look for communists,' a man joined in.

'Well, Ali isn't no communist. He belong *mos* to the mosque and he goes every Friday, don't I say?'

'Man, don't be so blerry stupid, *mos*, man. Don't you read the *koerant* then?'

'What papers?'

'I don't talk about it here, hey, political stuff. You can't open your jaw too much, according that walls got ears, *mos*.'

'*Ja*, there's a lot of blerry fif' columns working for the governmen'.'

'Blerry law is everywhere.'

The bus swayed and sagged along the road. Before it reached the main part of the suburb, Beukes reached out and pressed the bell, then extricated himself slowly from the crowd on the platform.

'Don't fall off, *ou* pal,' a man laughed.

Beukes stepped from the platform as the bus slowed down at the stop. He waited at the roadside, slightly dishevelled, and watched some traffic sweep past before he crossed quickly. Standing for a moment by the grass verge he looked back in the direction the bus had taken. He could see its lighted rear windows and the driving lights winking red, receding into the

70

dark distance. Francy is out there, he thought; old Francy, Francy, Francy. He realized that he had almost forgotten her, and love and nostalgia mingled for a while and walking along the footpath through the grass, he thought, why the hell am I doing this? Why the hell? But he threw off the thought a little reluctantly, discarding it like a favourite coat, and went on along the road, carrying the cheap case packed with illegal handbills. He thought instead of their distribution and his meeting with Hazel.

CHAPTER SIX

Hazel was the code name for Elias Tekwane. When he was born his mother had really named him after his great-grandfather, but some years later when she had taken him to learn to read and write at the mission down the track from the village, past the old bluegum tree in which the children had made a swing, the missionary, who always found it difficult to pronounce indigenous names, had said: 'We'll call him Elias, that's a nice biblical name.'

Elias went to classes at the mission when he was not driving the family's two cows out to graze on the scrubby hillside behind their house with the boys from other families. That was a man's work, while the womenfolk mostly worked the fields.

The rains came in October and November in that part of the country. Then the ploughs were brought out to prepare the soil for planting. Throughout the winter the soil was dry and dusty and when the cattle went through the fields they munched the abandoned maize stalks, leaving only dust. Then the wind carried the dried leaves from the maize stalks and they whistled as they blew through the air, whistled as they scratched at faces and legs, and cut the dry skin.

But the ploughing season was the best. It was spring; the sun began to rise early and the yellow light lay on the land like a bright, wrinkled sheet in the mornings. The sounds of life emerged with the early sunlight: the shrilling of the wheels on the ox-drawn ploughs, the pop of a whip, bird songs and the songs of children, the hallooing of many voices.

With the harvest, before the sun went down over the sharp brown hills, lines of women and girls could be seen trudging towards the town, carrying loads of corn in paraffin cans on their heads or in sacks on their backs. The corn was sold in the town for sugar, salt, tea, and to pay the taxes. When the crop was poor there would be debt with the White shopkeeper.

When the sun set in that part of the country, the sky in the west turned yellow and orange and green, and the straggling clouds hung like tattered tinsel from the rafters of the sky. The houses of the village lay on the hillsides like discarded toys on a rumpled carpet of brown and ochre. The scene looked as pretty as a postcard to any newcomer or passer-by.

Elias could not remember his father, and knew of him only from things his mother told him. But one day he knew that his father was dead and that he would never see him again. News arrived that Tekwane had been killed in a mining accident near Johannesburg; he was buried hundreds of feet below ground, deeper than any of his ancestors had been buried. After that, each month Elias's mother went into the town to the post office to collect what she called 'The Pension' of two pounds which the mine paid to her for her husband's life.

At the mission school Elias progressed fairly well; he could do simple arithmetic and spelling. When he was not in the little corrugated iron classroom or tending the cattle, he and the other children of the village played around the old bluegum tree, swinging from the rope tied to a lower branch. Sometimes they would walk all the way to the railway line through the scrub and the crumbling, eroded land that turned to powder under their cracked feet.

Frequent visits to the railway eventually brought about the realization that the trains passed at certain times, so that the children knew almost exactly when the train going north would pass, and the time of the southbound one. According to this rough timetable they would gather at the railway lines to wait for the trains.

Sitting under the thorn trees, which were brown and withered as an old woman's hands, they would wait for the sound of the whistle. The first hoot always came from far off, as if an owl scouted a long way out along the line of scrub-covered hills. From where the boys sat the hills looked like the

73

thin form of a starving girl covered by a thin blanket: you could make out the shape of the insignificant breasts, the meagre belly and the bony knees.

Slowly the train would come into sight, wheezing and puffing up the grade like the old missionary when he was annoyed. First came the locomotive, long and heavy with its smoke-stack like a top-hat, and the huge wheels of iron clanking away as steam belched; in the cabin would be two *amabulu,* White men, with minstrel-blackened faces and sweat rags about their throats. Then the heat-blasting rumble was past and next came the carriages, a long line of them, clacking and snapping as the couplings lurched into each other.

The children would run with the train, cheering and waving their hands. The passengers in the carriages would be looking out at the stunted trees and the parched gullies that gashed the ground like yellow wounds, and at the hills that gave a ragged edge to the flat blue sky. Sometimes packets of half-eaten food were tossed out to the shrieking children and when the train had passed, whistling into the sun-scorched distance, they would turn back panting, to gather the jettisoned leftovers. There would be partly-bitten sandwiches, broken biscuits, some chicken bones with a little meat left on them sticky with jam from crumbled cakes, burst oranges and chipped candy.

One afternoon Elias's mother returned from the post office and he heard that 'The Pension' was finished. The mine had awarded her forty pounds compensation, to be paid at two pounds a month, and that day she had been told that she had drawn the last of it the previous month. Of course, the mine had neglected to tell her, among other things, that the widows of White miners killed alongside her husband had been awarded fifteen pounds a month for the rest of their lives.

*

Baas Wasserman's shop was the most popular in the little

town. You could buy almost anything there, from packets of coffee to heavy, grease-covered parts of motorcars or farming machinery. There were shelves stacked with groceries and sweets and racks stocked with folded blankets, khaki trousers and heavy boots. There were also some cut-glass bowls and vases but very few of these were sold and they stood on the shelves gathering dust. The front of the shop was decorated with advertisements for tobacco and ginger-pop, and the verandah, which had to be swept clean every morning and afternoon, was shaded by a corrugated iron roof.

The White people went in and out of the store as they pleased, but the Blacks could only be served through a square hole cut in the side wall facing the yard. Usually the customers on that side had to wait a long time to be served when there were White people making purchases inside because, apart from attending to them, Wasserman's wife also carried on interminable conversations and sometimes offered a favourite customer coffee or a bottle of mineral water.

While they waited, the Black shoppers usually teased Elias who swept the front of the store, calling him the new boss of the place, or enquiring after the size of the profit made the day before.

'We see you, little boss. And how was the business yesterday?'

'A lot of money,' Elias would reply, grinning at the faces grouped at the end of the verandah.

'How! Then it is possible to get something a little cheaper today. A sack of flour should cost less than it did yesterday, not so, little boss?'

'Certainly, granny, you may have as much flour as you want for no money at all.'

'The ancestors bless you, but you are a kind little man. But I do not think this Wasserman would agree, eh?'

'No, I do not think so.'

'Nevertheless, he showers his money upon you for keeping the shop clean, eh?'

'I also help to clean the house behind the shop, and cut the firewood.'

'How! Then he must pay you in diamonds.'

'I get three shillings and sixpence every Friday, granny.'

'Hi, hi, hi, what wealth! Three shillings and a sixpence!'

Behind the house was what used to be a stable and there Wasserman stowed all the odds and ends for which he no longer had any use. He threw nothing away. The stable was the roost of abandoned cartwheels, broken bedsprings, discarded cupboards crushed into splintering polygons of wood, rusty cans and empty petrol drums, a spade with a broken handle, broken mirrors with leprous faces and an infinity of unidentifiable metal and wooden contraptions gathering dust and rust. It appeared as if all the left-overs of several lives had been hastily crammed into the place.

Exploring this accumulation of driftwood from several existences one day, Elias came across an upset pile of damp and mouldy books. He had already pocketed a brass doorknob and a pocket knife with a broken blade. Under the grime of the knife's embossed handle he had discovered tiny scrollwork covered with raised lettering and the face of a man whom he later identified as Paul Kruger.

Now he paged over the clammy books. Most of the printing had been obliterated by damp and mildew, but he discovered that one of them was reasonably legible. There were pictures here and there, soggy line drawings of White men in heavy masks on horseback carrying shields and spears. Others were firing arrows into the distance. The pictures puzzled him: he had always identified spears and shields and field battles with his own people. The old men in the village often recounted the history of the people to an audience of children and younger men and women, and from their voices Elias could hear the thudding feet, the rattle of spears against shields, and the war cries. But here was a book showing White people doing the same things, fighting in the same way, except for the addition of the horses.

The thought entered his mind that possibly the Whites were the same as his people, except that their skin was different. Well, it seemed to be proven here: the decorated shields, the clubs, the lances. Elias examined the front of the book – it had no cover – and spelled out the title: *The White Company*. He struggled with a damp line, *How Hordel John came . . .* He secreted the book happily under his shirt. In the evening he took home his discoveries, the doorknob, the embossed knife-handle, and the book, along with other left-overs of food given him by Mevrou Wasserman: one existed on left-overs.

In the evenings he puzzled over the book, struggling with the words. It was certainly an exciting book; there were battles, travels and adventures. Of course all these things had taken place many, many years ago, he discovered, but the places described must still exist – unknown, mysterious places beyond the village, Wasserman's shop, the bluegum tree, the locomotive clanking up the grade and the packets of bitten sandwiches lying in the dry, brittle grass around the thorn bushes.

As the days passed Elias grew hard and sturdy. He was bull-shouldered and tough in the arms and legs. At fourteen he even sprouted a faint moustache which made him giggle, and the older ones mocking called him 'Man'. He still owned the broken pocket-knife which he had polished bright with spittle and a rag – the doorknob he had presented to his cousin. The knife and the book he refused to part with, not that there was any great demand for the book. He had finally mastered the long tale and re-read it several times and sometimes when he spoke in the language of the book, he was called a 'Black Englishman' by the White children who passed by the village or Wasserman's shop.

The old missionary who had first taught him to read and write had gone, and a younger man had been sent in his place. This one had a heavy grey moustache and elderly eyes that held the sadness of an old hound. He was not very popular in the town, being inclined towards the English language, but since he concentrated on bringing religion to the village and did not get in the way of the more rabid Afrikaners, he was tolerated. From him Elias learned that people no longer spoke English in the manner of the book, and he was also assisted by him with arithmetic when he was not at Wasserman's store.

Then came a time when the people in the town and the village learned of the War. This wasn't a war of shields and charging cavalry, Elias learned. Neither was it like the Boer War of which the old people knew. Also, the war was being fought overseas, in Europe – he knew of France and England from the book – but it had now spread to North Africa. Even more interesting was the fact that the Government had committed the country on the side of the English in this war, and men were being recruited into the army.

The Whites in the town, most of them, were angry about this. They sympathized with the Germans who were fighting the English and were killing the Jews. They even called a meeting in the school-house in the town to complain about the Government's decision. 'To hell with the red-necked English,' they cried. 'And as for the Jews, well, let Hitler kill the whole bloody lot of them. All they do is get rich at other people's expense and bring foolish ideas into the minds of the kaffirs.' But nothing came of their meeting, and they gave up, grumbling.

A recruiting team came to the town to sign on men. A few of the younger Whites who did not agree entirely with their elders joined up. But even more startling was that the army was also signing on Africans. The recruiting team turned up near the village with a brand-new armoured car for display and a camouflaged truck. There were two White sergeants in khaki and several African soldiers with brass elephants on their hats. African men were needed to carry stretchers and to work as cooks and cleaners: the Government did not allow them to bear arms, but they were needed to do the menial work of war.

For Elias this presented an opportunity to tread beyond the boundaries of the village. But when he presented himself for recruitment, a black soldier threw back his great head and neighed with laughter like an old horse, slapping his khaki thighs and crying, '*Hi, hi, hi, hamba, hama, piccanin.* Go away, little boy. What? Do you think that you can win the war for us? You think that the Germans will flee in terror at the sight of you? No. Come back again when you have another foot length in your legs and you have become a man.' The other soldiers laughed with him and the White sergeants chuckled. Elias turned away, thinking that perhaps the people in the town were right in disagreeing with the war.

But when he related the incident, laughing inwardly, to Wasserman, the shopkeeper became incensed. His red neck, scrawny and rugose as a turkey's, twitched and throbbed with rage and his mouth squirmed like a worm in a puddle, while his eyes bulged like peeled eggs. 'How dare you,' he squeaked. 'How dare you, a little no-good kaffir, interest yourself in the business of White people? You *verdomde* black things are becoming too cheeky. So they are taking black things to fight their war, yes? And when you come back you want to be like us. I hope the whole lot of *bliksems* smother in the dirt. And as for you, you *niks-niks* locust, you can clear off and don't let me see you again.'

After this incident Elias returned to the stony field on the hillside behind the village, joining the other herd-boys, or he would thrust the plough-blade into the crusty earth, whooping at the old ox that stumbled ahead. He and his mother lived on the anaemic ears of corn which the land yielded, on a sinewy chicken now and then, on the remains of meals begged in the town, and on the kindness of the village community. Anger grew inside him like a ripening seed and the tendrils of its burgeoning writhed along his bones, through his muscles, into his mind. Why, he thought, why, we are as they are, except that their lands are bigger and they have more money, and all we do is work for them when we are not trying to make a little corn grow among the stones of our own patches.

As the war progressed there came a need for men to work in the big cities and labour recruiting teams came into the

79

reserves where the black folk lived to contract workers. The young men were forced to contract themselves, for the debts with the shopkeepers had grown and the land did not provide enough to pay them and feed the families.

Elias offered himself, having first registered for a pass because, naturally, in order to leave one's home one had to have the permission of the White authorities.

*

When African people turn sixteen they are born again or, even worse, they are accepted into the mysteries of the Devil's mass, confirmed into the blood rites of a servitude as cruel as Caligula, as merciless as Nero. Its bonds are the entangled chains of infinite regulations, its rivets are driven in with rubber stamps, and the scratchy pens in the offices of the Native Commissioners are like branding irons which leave scars for life.

'Where is your pass, kaffir?'

'It is here.'

'Ah, I see that you are from such and such a place. Where is your permission to travel from there?'

'It is here.'

'Good. Now having permission to travel from such and such a place, where is your permission to be in *this* place?'

'It is here.'

'Ah. Now having had permission to move from such and such a place and again having permission to be in this place, where do you work?'

'I work here, for such and such a man.'

'Good. Excellent. Do you have a permit to work for such and such a man?'

'It is here.'

'Ah, yes, I see. It is all written here and stamped and this such and such a man for whom you work has signed regularly each month. Good, excellent, everything is perfect. But, tell me, where exactly do you live in this place?'

'In such and such a location, township, street, alley or hole in the ground.'

'Marvellous. Now, living in such and such a location, municipal township, street, alley, hole in the ground, do you have the necessary permission signed, sealed and stamped?'

'It is here.'

'Wonderful. You have everything: permission to exist as shown by the fact that you have registered with the authorities; permission to leave the place of your previous existence; permission to arrive in *this* place and remain here by the grace of God and the Native Commissioner; you have permission to work for such and such a man; you have permission to live at such and such a location. Tell me, are you married?'

'Yes.'

'Where is your wife, your children?'

'They are at the place where I existed previously.'

'Good. Remember, they cannot come to live with you or to visit you without first gaining permission. Not to do this would be to invoke the wrath of the Devil and all his minions.'

'I will remember.'

'Good. Naturally, while having permission to come to this place from such and such a place in order to visit you, it is necessary that your wife, your children, your uncles, aunts, grandfathers and grandmothers, all the sundry who wish to *live* with you, should have permission to do so. You understand, of course.'

'I understand.'

'By the way, you also understand that you are not allowed to leave the job with this man in order to take up another job with someone else, without permission?'

'It is so.'

'Marvellous. You are a good kaffir. You understand, of course, that you are not allowed to travel from here to take up residence in another place without first having permission to leave here and arrive there? And to remain there, take up residence, to work, to go to work and to return from work, to walk out at certain times, and so on and so forth also requires permission.'

'I understand.'

'You are a wizard if you are able to understand. But understand one thing.'

'What?'

'If these things are not followed with care, then into the prison with you or all permits cancelled so that you cease to exist. You will be nothing, nobody, in fact you will be decreated. You will not be able to go anywhere on the face of this earth, no man will be able to give you work, nowhere will you be able to be recognized; you will not eat or drink; you will be as nothing, perhaps even less than nothing.'

'I understand.'

'So be it.'

CHAPTER SEVEN

On one side of the street the garden-fronted houses of artisans and the lower middle classes passed by, displaying a succession of name-plates: Montrose, Chez Nous, Nevada, Casa Loma, Sorrento. Banality went in the guise of exoticism; metal polish brought on a fantasy of far-away places. Behind the hedges and the honeysuckle creepers, lighted and curtained windows sang mutedly with radiophonic voices. The street-lamps gleamed like spilled syrup on the red-glazed garden paths, while on the other side of the street, as if ashamed of its intrusion, a brick schoolhouse shrank back in the gloom behind a wire fence and partly obscured the moon.

Beukes was back in the past, whisked there by the time-machine of memory, and he saw himself, seven years old, going to school for the first time. Once upon a time he had worn a little blue cap and had carried a slate in one hand while his father had held the other, escorting him into the grounds of the school, red brick and tiled roof, on the hillside above the city. There had been many windows and they had made the school look vast.

It had been a school for Coloureds and the massed faces of children had formed a conglomerate pattern of various shades of brown, from light tan to chocolate, as they had wriggled and writhed restlessly. The monotonous chanting of multiplication tables had droned along the corridors: 'One and one is two, two and two make four ...' Those had been the years of primary readers, the fables of Aesop, the Cruel Queen and long division, the rehearsal for the annual concert.

They had been told that they would be giving a special performance of their concert for a White school. That was really the first time that the little boy had realized that children

83

called 'White' attended separate schools. As the crocodile of child performers had made its way through the streets to another part of the city, he had wondered fearfully whether they would make a good showing at this new, strange place. Perhaps the White children would laugh at them. He was a lawyer in the children's play and had to wear a cotton wool wig and satin gown: 'Gentlemen of the jury, with me you must agree; return, I pray, a verdict that will set the prisoner free.'

But now he was alone in the suburban street with the residue of childhood clinging like candy-floss, and his footfalls made harsh, scratchy sounds on the asphalt of the sidewalk. Loneliness stretched away behind and ahead of him, flanked on one side by ornate doorknobs and terra-cotta walls, and he was once more holding the cheap cardboard case full of illegal handbills with the anxious air of a traveller suddenly put off at a strange, half-lit town from which all humanity had mysteriously fled. When he finally turned through a gate towards a doorway of half stained-glass, it was with a sense of relief, of arrival.

Overhead a plant hung in a wire net and dangled dark tendrils which caressed his face like an alien thing. Somewhere inside the house, beyond the stained-glass, voices were raised in argument. There was life behind the illuminated design of fleur-de-lis and leaded quarterings. He stood in the frosted glow of coloured light and pressed the brass-and-porcelain bell-button. Inside a buzzer made an incongruous clattering. The arguing voices of young people went silent.

After a few moments the big porcelain knob turned and the door was opened by a teenage girl in shorts and shirt with hair in curlers. She looked out at him from a background of polished hallway.

'Good evening, sir.'

'Mister Flotman, please,' Beukes said, smiling down at her. He stood there with the cardboard case and ordinary brown suit and smiled at her with the long upper-lip. Nubile eyes gazed curiously at him in turn, hesitating for a moment.

Then, 'Mister Flotman? Yes, he's inside,' the girl told him. She stepped aside to admit him and from the direction of the kitchen a tall, bony woman with a face like a burned biscuit and neat clothes moved forward with the quiet manner of a nun. She even held her brown, knotty hands in the position of prayer – or was it washing-up?

The girl said, 'Gennelman for Mister Flotman, Missus Harris.'

'Oh, yes,' the woman said. 'You go back to your room, Thelma.' It was her duty to keep her female charges out of the reach of predatory males – responsibility had made her cautious; matriculation took precedence over matrimony. To Beukes she said, 'The name?'

'Hendricks,' Beukes lied easily. 'A friend of Henry's.'

He stood in the hallway and the girl shut the door behind him. A youth in summer shorts came out of a room and said crossly to the girl: 'I tell you, you did take my dividers.'

The girl said, '*Gwan*, you're mad,' and stuck a pink tongue out at him.

'Stop that,' the landlady commanded, and they went off, resuming the argument, while the dark woman led the way a little distance down the hall and opened another door. 'He's in here, Mister Hendricks.' She looked into the room, 'A Mister Hendricks for you.'

A voice asked, 'Hendricks? What Hendricks?'

But Beukes skilfully was inside the small, cluttered room, winking at the man there who grinned and nodded. 'Oh, yes, Hendricks, yes. Thank you very much, Missus Harris.'

He was sitting in a stuffed armchair, a marking-pencil in one hand and an exercise book on one knee, surrounded by the battlements of education: toppled rows of encyclopaedias, *The Decline and Fall of the Roman Empire*, piled and dog-eared journals, numerous school text-books. Afrikaans poetry stood cheek-to-cheek with Sir Walter Scott and an old dressing-gown partly concealed the Peloponnesian Wars.

Beukes went to him and shook the hand that still held the

85

pencil. Flotman said, 'Jesus. Hendricks, Hendricks. The last time you came to see me – at the school – it was Abrahams or Ackerman or something.'

'I'd forgotten,' Beukes told him. 'How is it with you?'

'You should tell me,' Flotman said. 'Sit down, man.' He looked at the pencil in his hand, put it down, tumbled the war between Sparta and Athens onto the floor and rolled up the dressing-gown. 'How are things?'

Beukes sat on the rediscovered chair and putting the case down beside it he searched for a cigarette. In another part of the house youthful voices were again raised in altercation. Flotman sat in the stuffed chair, holding the bundled gown on his knees. He said, 'Man, I will not give up the suspicion that our Missus Harris deliberately and sadistically runs one boarding-house for both teachers and pupils.'

'What's new?' Beukes asked while Flotman produced the lid of a tin can as an ashtray.

'Nothing. I am still bewilderedly trying to drum the causes of the bloody Napoleonic Wars into sundry thick skulls.' He looked sour and went on. 'Not that I'm browned off by failure. Oh, no. If you knew what we have to teach these days, you wouldn't worry if nobody absorbed the stuff. Do you know that we are told to teach that everything that happens is ordained by God and that it's no use, even sinful, trying to change the order of things. The Boer War was a sort of holy crusade, evolution is heresy and nobody existed in this country before Jan Van Riebeeck arrived. In our segregated, so-called universities, modern psychology is a cardinal sin.'

'Befogging the mind,' Beukes said. 'It helps them. Unfortunately our teachers have to participate in this indoctrination.'

'I'm going to have to give up one day,' Flotman sighed. He was a squat man with a face like a badly formed and stale cheese, flat, round and yellowish, flat of nose and broad of cheekbone. 'It's like banging your head against a wall, man.'

Smiling, Beukes said, 'The wall will cave in one day. Your

86

head is hard enough.' He blew smoke and gazed at the teacher through the drifting grey threads. 'You ought to get married,' he said. 'A woman gives a bloke comfort, even the thought of having one somewhere.'

Flotman said, 'Tchah. But I admire the way you boggers go ahead. Nothing seems to stop you. What drives you?'

'Drives? Nothing drives us,' Beukes replied. 'We understand our work, so we enjoy it. It is rarely that one is happy in one's work.'

'You go to jail, you get beaten up by the fascist police. All right, all right, no lecture is required. But Jesus Christ, don't you baskets ever get fed up?'

'Some of us do, I suppose,' Beukes said. 'But why do you say "you"? Are *you* somebody apart?' Beyond the room, in another region, the children still argued over lost dividers.

'I'm scared.' Flotman admitted, 'I don't want to go to jail and eat pap and lose my stupid job or get bashed up by the law. In the last few years hundreds of our teachers have taken exit-permits and have gone overseas. Why do I stay on? Am I like you? I could be teaching in Canada. I'm not like you. Your heart is too big, Beukes. Too big.' He shook his head and then looked up again. 'But what can I do to ease my conscience once more? That's what you're here for, isn't it – Mister Hendricks?' He discovered that he was still holding the bundled dressing-gown and put it aside on a pile of exercise books.

Beukes indicated the case at his feet. 'We have some leaflets to be handed out. Tomorrow night, the same as last time.' He named an area nearby.

'Okay, okay,' Flotman said. 'If I can't teach history to my young students, at least I can get them to help make it in some small way.'

'They're safe, of course?' Beukes asked, taking up the attache case. 'You're not using *them*?' He motioned towards the sounds of argument.

'Lord, no! Young nuisances, man. My boys and girls are

slightly older and from other parts.' He grinned, adding, 'One does not operate in the territory where one lives – they have taken to surreptitious reading of the theories of guerilla warfare under the flaps of their desks. Don't worry, they're safe. They weren't caught last time. *They* don't want to get bashed up either, or charged with subversion.'

'They must be careful,' Beukes said. 'You can be arrested and put away indefinitely, just on suspicion.'

'Okay, okay, pal,' Flotman said, chuckling. 'We're not *that* stupid, even though we're budding intellectuals.'

Beukes laughed quietly. 'You're a joker,' he said. 'A great joker.' Then he added seriously, 'But there is also the matter of political education for these young people. I will see that you get more material for them, as soon as I can lay hands on some. Prohibited stuff is scarce.'

There was a tap on the door and Flotman got up and went to open it while Beukes put down the case again as Mrs Harris came in, carrying a tray of tea and biscuits like a votive offering. Behind her the altercation still went on.

She smiled at Beukes. 'I'm sure you'd like some tea. It cools a person in this weather.'

'You shouldn't have bothered,' Beukes told her, with his hands on the attache case.

Flotman was lumbering about and looking wildly around for a place to set the tray. He decided upon a corner of the desk and swept away a stack of exercise-books. While Mrs Harris was putting down the tea things, Beukes read from a page on the floor: 'The *voortrekkers* wanted to go on keeping slaves and did not agree with the emancipation, so they decided to trek into the interior of the country. They were led by men like Hendrick Portgieter . . .'

Mrs Harris was asking, 'Is Mister Hendricks also a teacher?'

Beukes looked up and Flotman said quickly, 'No, no, Missus Harris, Mister Hendricks goes around selling encyclopaedias. He's trying to sell me a set, but I don't think I need one.'

Mrs Harris said clucking, 'Oh, what a shame. It must be quite a tiring job, hey? Do you go from door to door?'

'Er-not really. Only to those people I think might be interested,' Beukes replied, smiling up at her.

'Well, good luck then,' the landlady said as she moved towards the door. 'I must go and send those children off to sleep. They ought to be done with their homework by now.' She smiled at Beukes and went out, shutting the door behind her.

When she had gone, Flotman said, 'Just like a mother, that woman, although she terrifies me. Have a biscuit?' He passed a cup of tea to Beukes who put it aside on top of a pile of books.

'Encyclopaedias,' he chuckled, holding a sugary biscuit.

'Well, you do, sort of, don't you?' Flotman asked innocently.

He stirred his tea while Beukes absently put the biscuit in his pocket and opened the case, extracting packets of handbills. 'Tomorrow night,' Beukes said. 'Can you arrange it? Damn short notice, but it's got to be done. They must all go out at the same time. That disperses the chances of getting nabbed. At . . .'

'It's all right, pal,' Flotman said with his mouth full of biscuit. He drank his tea noisily and then put the cup aside and examined a handbill. He had thick, heavy hands, like a workman's. 'Hmmm, hot stuff, hey. If you get caught with this stuff, it's the high jump.' He waved it at Beukes. 'Don't worry, don't worry. My young folk are very reliable, even if they have an abhorrence for the Treaty of Vienna.' He drank some more tea. 'Some of the young ones are inclined to be pretty romantic about revolution, but their hearts are in the right place . . . Your tea is getting cold.' Chuckling, '*They* are getting plenty nervous, especially since the fighting started up north. The Minister made a pompous speech. Of course, the newspapers are agreed to play down the whole thing, give the army and police all the victories. To think only some years ago we were holding meetings, marches, passive resistance.'

'There's no point in talking violence if you can't put it into effect,' Beukes said, sipping his tea which had cooled and was now tasteless. He put the cup aside and picking up his case, stood up, smiling at the teacher. 'Well, I must be moving on with my encyclopaedias.'

Flotman asked, 'Are you going? We could have a drink, now that Missus Harris won't be coming back. There's a bottle of port somewhere.' He gazed about the broken terrain of books and furniture.

'Don't bother,' Beukes said. 'It makes me sleepy and I have to keep awake tonight. Some other time, hey, pal.' He added, 'You will see to those handbills, okay?'

'Not to worry,' Flotman told him, getting up too. 'We bloody teachers need to help. We have talked about the revolution among ourselves too long. All very intellectual. Okay, Buke, not to worry, man.' He patted the other man's shoulder. 'I'll see you to the door.'

Out in the hallway all was quiet. Mrs Harris had put an end to the juvenile squabbling and the silence of a shut chapel hung in front of the stained-glass window, so that they automatically advanced towards the door on tip-toe. From outside the warm air of the summer night pushed in and Beukes felt it on his face like a sweaty hand. He turned to the schoolmaster and said softly, 'See you then, man.'

'See you, brother,' Flotman whispered, but went with him out into the open as far as the gate. He stood at the gate, looking down the street until he could no longer see the other man in the darkness and the sound of footsteps on the paving had faded away. Then he turned back towards the house, feeling a little sad.

CHAPTER EIGHT

The sewing-machine went brrrt-brrrt-brrrt each time the woman trod on the pedal. She worked under an electric standard lamp that made her dark Indonesian face look lighter, and her ringed fingers guided the material skilfully under the darting needle. On a table bright cloth made a pyramid, and the floor around her was scattered with offcuts and pieces of thread. With most of the light concentrated around the sewing-machine the rest of the room was dimly lit, the furniture in shadow: a big settee, two easy-chairs with the upholstery on the arms frayed and the backs stained by the oil from resting heads and a glass-topped coffee table with snapshots stuck under the glass for display, the walls were decorated with mirrors engraved with texts from the Koran in gold paint.

'Abdullah did say he was going to be home early tonight,' the woman said, licking the end of a thread of cotton. 'I don' know what is keeping him now. Maybe he had to go and see the folk at the kerom club. People don' play kerom so much no more, but Abdullah and his boys, they keep it going, mos. Dominoes and draughts and kerom. Sunday mornings there is a whole to-do when they get together.' She threaded the needle expertly and worked the wheel of the sewing-machine with one hand. 'It keep them mos out of mischief. But maybe he will be here any minute now.'

'Oh, I'm not in a great hurry, thanks,' Beukes said from the settee. He had been waiting for more than half-an-hour and he was already bored and tired. The room was warm and close. He sat there in the springy enclosure of frayed brocade breathing in the faint scent of dead joss sticks, not saying much, allowing the woman to go on talking while she worked.

'I must finish this dress tonight, so it will mean whole

night working,' she said. She smiled and Beukes noticed that she had several gold teeth in her dentures. The machine shirred on. 'The customer is going to Port Elizabeth tomorrow and she want the dress to take with her. Then I still got to make finish a wedding dress for a girl what's going to get married on Saturday. Busy, busy, busy.' Brrt-brrrt-brrrt went the machine. 'I get a lot of work from White people. They is blerry fussy, but I charge them extra, the damn cheats. They can afford it, is it not right? Evening gowns, wedding gowns, cocktail dresses. Halima, they say to me, I want you must finish this dress by the week-end because why I must go to a reception with my husband. Or, I got to go to the Mayor's gar'en party, hey. Yes, merrem, I say, but I think in my mind, you go to sleep, you White rubbish. All they know is order you about, so I put on an extra two or three pounds on the price. Let them pay if they want to chase one on. What would they do without us people? Where will they get dressmakers, servants, people to work for them? Nice living they got, with a lot of black people to do the work. And look how they treat us. Isn't I right, mister?'

'You're dead right,' Beukes said to her from the other part of the room, feeling heavy-eyed.

He sat there, abandoned, in his cheap brown suit, the maroon tie, the brogues, while time bobbed by, measured in reels of cotton, lengths of material, while the dressmaker chattered on behind her machine. Between his feet stood the cardboard case with its cargo of illegal handbills, carefully guarded even in the presence of the gold-painted blessings of Allah and the faded aroma of stale incense.

He thought, sleepily, that he would like to go home to Frances. He was back again on that Saturday afternoon, long ago, when he'd climbed the inscribed stairway of the dreary block of municipal flats, past the washlines and the flat vista of grass worn in patches like the coat of an old dog, the rows of single-storey council cottages like frayed uniforms. When he'd reached her door he had felt nervous, and had knocked apprehensively. From inside he had been able to hear the Saturday sports commentator describing a rugby match on the radio.

He had knocked again with reckless vigour and somebody inside had called out to another, against the crowd-roar and the commentator's excited voice. Then the door had been opened and from behind the elderly woman who had opened it the crowd noise had surged and the commentator had screamed hysterically, '... passes - the - ball - to - Vanderwalt -and - Vanderwalt - heads - for - the - touchdown - looks - like - he's - going - to - make - it - he's going - to - make - he's - going - to - make - it - yes - he's - going - to - make - it - HE'S - MADE - IT - HE'S - MADE - IT,' while the crowd had roared excitedly.

'Oh, good afternoon,' the grey-haired woman had smiled. 'You must be the young man for Frances.' She had turned and shouted back into the flat, 'Daddy, turn down that wireless.' To Beukes: 'Frances's daddy listens to the rugby when he's not out on Saturdays. You must come in.'

In the parlour with its cheap, carefully-kept store furniture, a small, dried-out old man had sat in an armchair in front of the gram-radio, listening to the segregated football match. Reaching out he had turned down the sound to a murmur as his wife had ushered in Beukes.

'Sit down,' she had told the young man. 'This is Frances's father.' The old man had nodded at him, and Beukes had had the feeling that he was accustomed to young men calling upon his daughter; that he, Beukes, was another in a long line of suitors. But the mother had said, 'I donno why Frances takes so long in the bathroom.' She had seemed eager that her daughter should appear, as if she was determined that this would be the last time, that Frances should now settle down and make a permanent arrangement. So she had bustled off to find her in another part of the flat.

Beukes had sat in a straight chair and had said, 'You don't have to turn it down for me, sir. You go on listening.'

93

The old man had searched for something in his coat pockets. 'It is okay. I mostly go to see our own people, but today's matches have been put off.' He had motioned towards the muted radio. 'These Boers can play rugby, I reckon, but it's about the only thing they do properly. You like rugby?'

Beukes had replied, 'Well, I'm more of a soccer man, though I haven't played since schooldays.'

'I like soccer if it's good,' the old man had said, still searching through his pockets. 'But rugby has more action, man.' He had given up the hopeless search and had looked around the room. 'Marie,' he had cried, 'Where the devil is my pipe, hey? I can't find my pipe.'

'Good lord, man,' the mother had called from somewhere. 'Do I smoke your ridiculous pipe?'

Then out of a short stretch of passageway had come Frances. She had had a towel wrapped around her head and there had been soapsuds on her brown arms, and the young man had noticed with surprise how long-legged she was and how her small breasts had pulled up under the overall she wore, as she had rubbed her hair with the towel. There had been a knotted feeling in his stomach as he had come out of the chair, smiling.

She had wrinkled her nose at him and had said, 'There, I told you if you came too early I'd still be washing my hair.'

He had said, loving her, 'Well, at least I can see you with your paint off, too.'

Suddenly he was aware that the woman at the sewing-machine had stopped chattering, and looking at her he saw her kerchiefed head cocked, listening. Footsteps grated outside, then the front door rattled and there was somebody in the hallway.

'*Daar's h*y, there he is,' she said, and called: 'Is that you, 'Dullah?'

A man looked into the room, saying, '*Salaam aleikum.*' Then he saw Beukes sitting there on the settee. 'Hey, it's you, hey? Hullo, sir, I'm glad to see you again.'

He came into the room, olive-skinned, his hair black and

shiny as patent leather, holding out his hand and smiling. He had gold in his teeth too and a meaningless moustache, like an idle scrawl on a photograph; he wore a violently checkered sports jacket and neat dark trousers. He was a cutter in a garment factory and probably had his own clothes made there as well. Beukes had the amusing vision of furtive goings-on during the lunch break, or the machine hands clandestinely doing their own tailoring in between sewing for the company.

Shaking hands, Beukes said, 'How goes it then, *ou* Dullah?'

'Sorry to keep you waiting, hey,' Abdullah said. 'I had to go somewhere on the way home, *mos*.'

'Ah, is okay,' Beukes told him. 'I was talking to the missus.'

The woman said from behind the machine, 'The food is in the oven, Dullah. I made chops. You can give the mister some also; there's enough.'

'Don't bother about me,' Beukes said, but Abdullah was already taking him by the arm and gesturing towards the back of the house. He stooped to pick up the attache case then followed the olive-skinned man to the kitchen while behind them the machine went brrt-brrrt.

Abdullah removed his jacket and hung it on the back of a chair then set out plates and cutlery. They sat in the kitchen and ate curried chops while Beukes told him about the handbills. Over the kitchen range hung a picture of the Q'aba at Mecca.

Abdullah said, '*Ja*, is awright. Tomorrow night then. Halima don't know about it.' He winked. 'The less said the better, *mos*. But they will go out.' He gnawed a bone, using his fingers. 'Tell you what, I'll also take some to the faktry, don't I say? Then I leave them out in the canteen at night, so when the people come in the morning they find them. Will that be okay?'

'That will be Friday morning,' Beukes told him. 'I reckon that will be all right. They won't suspect you? There are informers all over nowadays.'

'Trap boys,' Abdullah said. 'I know. You can't trust to open your mouth to anybody. But is okay, man. I'm stupid, I got no sense. I'm just somebody working there, patting the girls' behinds, making jokes.' He winked again. 'Don't tell Halima. No, it will be awright.' He licked curry gravy from his fingers. 'If we can only organize the workers proper nowadays. Is a hard business not knowing who to trust.' He shook his head disconsolately. 'What we going to do, mister?'

'We have to risk talking to people,' Beukes said, pricking at a chop. He was not feeling very hungry and had joined Abdullah more out of politeness than relish. 'You can smell out the good ones. Why, I found you, didn't I? You're one; there must be others. If we worry too much about spies we'll get nothing done.'

'The union officials are scared too,' Abdullah said. He got up and went to the range. 'I'll make some coffee.' In the front room the sewing-machine whirred on.

'They're soft,' Beukes said. 'But we have to pass them by. We can't neglect the workers just because some official is scared. The workers have acted before in spite of stupid or cowardly officials. Once the workers have seen that they should make a stand, no silly official is going to get in their way.'

'Oh, of course, yes,' the olive-skinned man said. 'They done it before, like you say. The time of the big strike after they, the law, shot all those people. *Ya Allah,*' he said, suddenly angry. 'How can it be that they just shoot down people because they come and say, "Look we are not slaves, we only want our rights"? Just to give the order to shoot, just like that. Look, we are all humans, don't I say? Just to shoot people down like that.'

'It shows that they are becoming incapable of governing any longer. That is why we must press on,' Beukes told him. 'That is why every little thing we do helps.'

Abdullah poured coffee into the cups and smiled again, showing his gold fillings. *'Insh'allah,* we will do our best.'

CHAPTER NINE

On the morning of the big strike that the two men spoke about the light had taken a long time to come. It was as if time had become static and the earth lived through a night without change, the thin greyness towards the east remained inscrutable, chill and mocking and insipid as over-watered gruel. Overhead the black sky pressed down heavily, so that the dawn strained to edge it back, like a man digging in his heels and thrusting back with his shoulders to move a heavy wagon.

But the people knew Time, and in the Township lamps flickered into life like fairy lights. Here and there the lights came on behind shabby curtains, behind cardboard patches in the windows, a length of sacking holding out the cold, an old coat stuffed into a hole. The sky weighed down on the Township, dark and oppressive, but gradually the night surrendered and the dawn crawled in behind a thin mist like the smoke of war.

The Washerwoman was awake long before that time. She had made some coffee and sat drinking it sleepily on her shabby bed under the cardboard ceiling, ignoring the thin, cold, sterile fingers of morning that touched her big, comfortable thighs, warm from the blankets. She had a heavy bundle of washing to do that day, the grimy accumulation of four households, and she meant to start early.

Somewhere, in another part of the Township, sticks rattled along rusty corrugated iron fences.

The Bicycle Messenger was in the backyard of the collection of shanties, groping around his machine, making sure that the tyres had not softened during the night. He burned his fingers on a match and cursed roundly under his breath. From the shacks around him came the sounds of reluctant activity as the Township folk stirred to face another day.

Along the streets youths in ragged clothes and assortments of hats, caps and threadbare balaclava helmets were carrying word from house to house wherever they found a light.

The Outlaw watched carefully from the corner of the tumbledown house before he crossed the dark pathway. He was in no mood to be caught by the husband on his way home from night-shift. One found a piece and took it; complications were unprofitable. He darted into the black embrace of an alleyway. Made hard and cynical by a long record of illegalities, he was now thinking of breakfast and jars of beer, the woman already forgotten. Silent as a cat on soft sand, he passed the shack where the Child slept.

The Child turned in her sleep on the floor and dreamed that she did not have to go to the little one-roomed school where she had to sit on the floor all day, growing weary. Instead, she was on a great ship with smoke pouring from the chimney, as she had seen in a picture book, sailing away towards a butter-coloured horizon. In the only bed, her parents were throwing off old coats and mumbling protestingly that they had to rise at this time.

Skirting the edge of the Township, a dirt road joined the long black tape raised like a dyke which unreeled towards the Town where the factories and steel mills were. If you crossed the dirt road you arrived in a big open, trampled and bare field, and beyond it you saw the Police Station.

Lights burned all night in the Police Station. The Sergeant had come on duty at four a.m. and now he was sitting at his desk, drinking coffee from the top of a flask, blowing at the steam that rose from the surface. The Sergeant had a flabby, wrinkled face over hard bone, as if a loose, flexible rubber mask had been hastily dropped over a smaller wig-stand. His eyes were indeterminate grey, like drops of dirty water, and he had big pink hands. He kept his uniform neat and elegant and usually moved with the bearing of an old soldier, so that he

had the appearance of a Commanding General – which he some
times day-dreamed he was – rather than a mere Sergeant.

There was nothing in particular referring to the past night
in the Charge Book, so the Sergeant hoped for a pleasant day
ahead. But he could not help feeling uneasy and somewhat
displeased because of the persistent rumours which had been
filtering in from the Township. The whole black population of
the country had been called on to defy the country's laws; the
bloody kaffirs were going to burn their registration books;
the Government was about to make a statement on the
carrying of these pass-books; the Blacks were going to overrun
the White districts and butcher everybody in sight. It should
have happened yesterday, it was going to happen today, tomorrow, next week, next month – nothing seemed definite.
Rumours continued to circulate, some urgent, others ridiculous.

At about seven in the morning the first constables came in
from the night patrols. They signed in and then stood around
the lockers in the back of the station, unbuttoning their
greatcoats. The Sergeant leafed through the badly written
notebooks of these 'Bantu' constables.

He looked up irritably: 'I say, what is this about words
written up on walls?' He spoke in Afrikaans which was the
language of all White police.

'Well, they have been writing on the walls again, *meneer,*'
one of the Black policemen said.

'The same things? Those damn agitators, *bliksems.*'

Another constable said in a heavy voice, 'They say they are
going to throw away the passes today.'

'*Today?* Who, man?'

'They, the people.'

'There is another thing, *meneer,*' the first policeman said.
'The passes will be thrown away and nobody will work.'

The Sergeant looked worried and angry. For a moment he
felt that this business was going beyond police routine and that
the job was becoming too big for him. But he quickly thrust
this thought aside and substituted another: 'You are in com-

mand, you are a General and you are about to engage in war.' This thought brought a glow of contentment. He wished the White staff would hurry up and report in; they would be more definite, reliable.

The telephone startled him and he grabbed at it nervously. Then he pulled himself together and raised the instrument, stroking his whitish-blond moustache. On the other end of the line, the Central station in the Steel Town was asking him to look into the lack of workers arriving from the Township that morning. There had been news that the so-called strike was taking place that day; was this true? Only a few workers were arriving in the Steel Town from his direction. Other stations were looking into the matter at their end as well.

'Hold on,' the Sergeant said to Central. He looked around at the constables who were chatting in a corner. 'Hey, you *bliksems*, what is this about the people not going to work today?'

The policeman who spoke with a heavy voice said, 'Sergeant, there are people going to work.'

'Well, the boss in town says they are not.'

'*Meneer*, some are going to work.'

The Sergeant looked angry. '*Some*? You mean the rest are staying at home?'

'We are not sure,' another policeman said. 'Some are going, some are not.'

'Jesus Christus,' the Sergeant blasphemed. He looked at the telephone still in his hand, then said into it: 'Look, I will investigate and ring you back.' He put the telephone down with a clatter and turned to the constables. 'Go and take a look around the bus terminus,' he ordered. It was time to take the matter well in hand, he thought; this could be serious. One of the constables looked surly and went out past the desk.

The Sergeant looked at the map, which included the Township, on the wall across the room, rubbing his wrinkled, loose-skinned chin. The map pleased him: it gave one a feeling of superiority over and above one's station. With a map one could think in terms of deployment of companies, establishment of command and observation posts. For a moment he longed for a little box of coloured flags on pins, which he could stick into the map, showing positions of forces. But the shriek of brakes snapped him out of the reverie like a pea blown from a tube, and through the doorway he saw the patrol car skid to a dusty stop outside and the White constables climb out.

Beyond them the open ground outside the Police Station was becoming lighter as the sunlight seeped through, and further away the Sergeant could make out enemy territory clearly: a line of ruined cottages mingled with tin shanties, a solitary lavatory built long ago by the municipality, a donkey grazing around a rubbish-heap.

In the Township the word had gone around for the surrender or destruction of all passes that day. The passes would be taken to the White man's Police Station and dumped there. There was some consternation and puzzlement: was not the anti-pass demonstration to take place next month? No, it would be today. But we are sure it is to take place next month – we are ready of course, but has the date been changed? *Away with the passes today. Everybody to the Police Station to dump the passes.* The White Government is going to make a statement about passes today. Who were calling on the people? A rival organization, *agents-provocateur,* the genuine leaders?

Some people went to work as usual, others stayed to take part in the manifestations. From today on, no more passes. Everybody to the Police Station to return the passes to the Whites.

Throughout the warming morning most of the population of the Township drifted towards the vacant lot in front of the Police Station. By midday a large crowd had gathered, shifting, ebbing, eddying, like a continuously disturbed puddle.

The Washerwoman was there – she had decided against the bundle of soiled clothes. She had brought her gay sunshade because it was going to be hot, and her face was plump and jolly below it.

There were elderly people, and children who had boycotted the schools that day; workers who had stayed away from the Steel Town, to show that they were tired of regimentation and chattels, of bullying police and arrogant foremen, of fines and taxes and having too little money with which to buy food. There were women, singing and swaying in the shade of umbrellas, and young girls giggling under the eyes of youths who strutted in black berets, patched trousers and ragged shirts.

The Bicycle Messenger had decided to strike too, and had purposely come on his cycle because it bore the name of his employer on the metal plate in the chipped frame.

There were others on bicycles edging about through the crowd. Many of the people were singing songs against the passes. Curiously, an atmosphere of holiday-making prevailed, and the 'Native Shop Number 5' on the nearest side of the Township was doing a brisk trade in ginger-pop and Coca Cola. A man who sold fat-cakes and coffee had set up his stall. Only the sky looked steely and ominous in spite of the sun, and some people predicted a thunderstorm.

As the sun moved westward, the crowd thickened. There was pushing, jostling, laughter. Those behind strained to see over the heads of those in front. People stood on tip-toe and craned their necks, shouting for news from those at vantage points. There was no news yet, or somebody was coming from the Steel Town to hear the complaints of the people. All the time cries were raised from the crowd while, 'Away with the passes,' and 'Down with pass laws,' groups were singing the old songs of struggle.

Instead of somebody to hear complaints a convoy of cars and trucks loaded with police reinforcements, plus an armoured car, came along the road from the Steel Town. The horns of the vehicles howled like starving animals forcing a way through the crowd, followed by hoots, jeers, catcalls and laughter. The cars, which carried senior officers of the Civil and Security Police and some journalists, went through the gate in the wire fence surrounding the Police Station, while the trucks and the armoured car were deployed at points around the open field. The crowd laughed and some went to examine the mud-coloured armoured car, as though they were visiting a military museum.

Inside the Police Station, the Sergeant realized that he had made a mistake. His face, wrinkled and flabby, now took on the aspect of an aged bloodhound. He had telephoned through to Central to report the gathering crowd, instead of taking command of the situation himself. He had surrendered the opportunity to prove himself a good General, to contain and eventually disperse the enemy. Even if they got out of hand, he had enough men, Sten-guns and Police Specials to deal with them, as well as *sjamboks* to drive them off like goats. Instead, he had made a grievous error and had practically called for help. So now he was no longer in command; the brass-hats, the gold-braid had arrived and he was nothing but another trooper – a non-commissioned officer, rather.

At about two in the afternoon an officer gave the command to load. The mechanisms of Sten-submachine guns and revolvers clacked and clicked with sounds of metallic efficiency. Dust rose from under the shuffling feet of the people who waited, some still singing, some calling out to one another, others chanting slogans.

The Outlaw was in the crowd. He had waited until the mass closed up so that he could ooze in quietly. Even among the poor there were pockets to pick, handbags to pilfer. He moved with the silent and unassuming slowness of oil among the various components of the crowd. Children jostled his legs but he took no notice of them. He smiled at strangers and winked at nubile girls, edged past youthful heads. He brushed past the Child who had come out of curiosity, disobeying the parental orders to remain at home while they attended the demonstration. The Child pushed past legs and crept about, hoping to get to the front where there should be a lot to see.

The crowd swayed and lumbered. Those behind pushed

those in front. There were protests, laughter, mild admonitions. Those in front were pushed against the wire surrounding the Police Station. Somebody was shouting, 'Take the passes, we don't want the passes.' Fists clutching the worn, brown reference-books were shaken aloft here and there. The hooting, singing, chanting, laughter went on. The sun was hot and the sky steely with thunder.

Then for some reason or another, a policeman shot into the noise. The sound of the shot was almost lost under the chanting, the singing, the laughter. Silence dropped from the gaping mouths of those who saw and heard, gaping in sudden wonder. Then there was a thin wailing and the front turned, the crowd surged back. Then all the police began to fire, a ragged volley at first. The crowd was already bursting away, scattering wide, a jumbled, falling, headlong rush away from the smoking iron muzzles of the guns; a wide-eyed fear, bewilderment, incongruous laughter from those who thought these were only warning shots. The firing burst out again like a roll of metal-skinned drums. From the front of the Police Station, from the groups around the trucks, from the turret of the armoured car, the shiny brass cylinders of spent ammunition leaped and cascaded for a moment in deadly ejaculations, and then stopped.

With the end of the volley came a silence of finality. Even the dogs of the Township did not bark. In the open field, in the dusty alleyways where they had tried to flee, the dead and the dying now lay like driftwood. The silence lay heavy and awkward for a while, until the wounded began to cry out for help. Then the stunned people drifted anxiously back to touch the dead and comfort the maimed.

A black preacher gave water to a man who moaned in shock, sitting in a puddle of his own blood; a toddler stood wonderingly over a heap of bloody clothes.

The police closed in, walking among the dead and wounded, while journalists clicked away with their cameras. At the Police Station some of the police who had fired looked at each other sheepishly, others looked out at the field with arid faces. The faces of the black policemen looked shamed under the khaki topis. The Sergeant was telephoning efficiently for ambulances, doctors, plasma, everything needed after a heavy assault.

The bundles of dead lay under the sun, with the abandoned pop bottles, fluttering pass-books, shoes, broken umbrellas, newspapers, all the debris of life and death. Among the dead was the Washerwoman. She had been shot low down while running away – the femoral arteries in the comfortable thighs had been torn through, so that she bled quickly to death, lying heaped on top of her collapsed sunshade by the runningboard of a parked car.

The Child lay on her face and there seemed hardly a mark on her, except when she was turned over and they saw the exit hole the heavy slug had made in the meagre chest. Her face was at peace and she seemed to be dreaming of something far away.

Those who found the Outlaw discovered that he took some time to die. He snarled up at those who tried to aid him, his life bubbling and frothing away through his mouth and nose and the neat line of holes punched through his back and lungs by most of the clip of a sten-gun.

The Bicycle Messenger had died instantly, sprawled joint-lessly over his fallen cycle which he had refused to abandon in flight, his flesh burst open, his spine shattered and his splintered ribs thrust into heart and lungs. One of his ankle clips had come off and was entangled in the spokes of a wheel.

While the living wandered, some aimlessly and others with purpose, among the dead and dying and wounded, the sky muttered darkly at last and started to shed heavy drops of rain. Thunder clashed along the horizon like a duel of artillery and then the rain began to fall steadily to mingle with the blood.

CHAPTER TEN

Soon, in spite of his long rest at Tommy's in the afternoon, Beukes was feeling sleepy again. Pausing on the corner of a street, he thought idly that it was curious that no matter how much you rested during the day when night came you automatically became sleepy. It was something to do with Pavlov's dogs, he had read somewhere, or something like that. Apart from sleepiness, he was also feeling physically tired: his legs ached and the soles of his feet burned in his brogues. The last bus had taken him far away from where he had wanted to be, so he had walked a long distance, and now he felt like sitting down on the edge of the pavement and resting his weary knees.

He yawned and felt in his coat pocket for a cigarette. His fingers touched something coarse and granular, and he drew out the biscuit which he had unconsciously placed in his pocket at Flotman's. He stood there in the half-light at the street corner alone, like a lost traveller, holding onto the cheap cardboard case as if it contained all his worldly possessions. Night had drained all life from this part of the city. It was as if the population had fled before an invasion of gloom from outer space, leaving everything behind: the dark houses with their cold windows, a bent signpost, an abandoned motorcar by the kerbside, the gaunt cat that slunk across the street, which looked back curiously at the man standing there, then disappeared. Overhead, the sky curved blackly and infinitely, its progress broken here and there by veils of cloud that pearled the stars.

Beukes stood there, resting his legs and crumbling the biscuit in his hand, feeling the crumbs trickle through his fingers like the beads of a rosary. Up ahead was the house where Isaac lived, a featureless place by day, now forlorn in the night, with its cracked steps leading up to the peeling double-doors, the big windows with their austere shutters, the drain-pipes coming apart. He tried to remember the rooms where Isaac lived with his mother and young sister, but could conjure up only a dusty piano with a dog-eared music book opened at *The Macabee's Chorus*; a portrait of one of their leaders now serving life imprisonment.

Carrying the case, now lightened of most of its contents, Beukes stepped off the pavement and crossed the dark street. In spite of fatigue he moved with the caution of someone grown used to hiding, to evading open spaces; the caution of someone who knew that a man alone in a street was as conspicuous as a pyramid, but that in a crowd one could become anonymous, a voice in a massed choir. So he kept to the deeper shadows of the walls, watching the street and the house ahead, hoping that Isaac had remembered to be home that night.

But Isaac wasn't home. Beukes was a few yards up the street when the girl spoke from the darkened doorway of a little shop. For a cold moment he heard the voice of the Security Police, chill, cynically triumphant, and his heart bumped within him. But it was a child's voice, the hushed voice of a girl, and looking into the doorway, his face still crawling, he saw the blurred smudge of her face, the wide anxious eyes, the outline of a gym dress. She stood there, a survivor of the plague of darkness, with her thin arms clinging to her midriff, saying in her hushed voice, 'Mister Beukes, that you, Mister Beukes?'

He stooped down and peered into the girl's ill-defined face. 'Ah,' he said quietly, 'it's Ike's sister, isn't it? What's happened, hey?' He knew that something was amiss and moved instinctively into the darkness of the doorway with her.

'What happened, hey?' He could hear her breathing. They stood close in the doorway in the dark, like lovers. 'Has something happened to Isaac?'

'I dunno, Mister Beukes,' the girl said. He could smell cheap perfume, lipstick, the child reaching impatiently out for woman-hood. 'I dunno, but Isaac, he never come home, and then he phoned here to the shop this afternoon and he said he wasn't coming home, and then the detectives came afterwards and searched the house. They were looking for Isaac, and shouted at my mummy. But we don't know where he is.'

She spoke breathlessly, hurrying to get the message out, like a radio-operator fumbling in his haste to tap out the SOS before the boilers blew and the ship went down with him. 'He said I was to keep watch for you because you might be coming to the house tonight and the detectives might be about, that I was to tell you they was looking for him and so he couldn't come home.'

Beukes felt cold. How could they have found out about Ike? But they seemed to be everywhere nowadays. He craned his neck and looked up and down the dark street. Somebody in Isaac's lot must have talked too much, or was a plant.

He asked, 'Did Isaac say anybody had been arrested or was also being looked for?'

'He didn't say nothing else, Mister Beukes.'

No, Ike wouldn't know; he had obviously cleared out as soon as he knew they were after him. But why were they after him now? They could have waited and caught him with Beukes and the illegal handbills – that way they would have a case for sure. Then they didn't know about him, Beukes, yet. They must have gone after Isaac on some other information received. The phrase was bitter in his mind: 'Information received'. But he would probably never find out.

It was all too haphazard, Beukes thought, standing there with the girl-child in the dark doorway, furtively, as if he was a child-molester. All too haphazard. Why, even the girl knew him. He thought of the child in the hands of the Bureau of State Security.

He asked, 'He didn't say he'd get in touch with me?' But he remembered Isaac would not know how; it was he who made contact with Isaac.

He could feel the girl's eyes anxious on his face in the gloom, more as if she thought she had failed by not gathering sufficient information, rather than that she wanted to get away, return home.

He smiled at her. 'All right, then. Thank you for waiting up all this time. Did you have to wait long?'

'It's nothing, Mister Beukes,' she said. 'My mummy said I had to wait until I saw you. Can I go now?'

'Of course, yes,' he replied. Then asked, smiling again: 'Do you still play the piano?'

She smiled shyly. 'Yes. I'm waiting for my examination results.'

'Good luck, then. Now you'd better get going, hey. Sorry you had to wait all this time.'

'Good night, Mister Beukes.'

She slid past him, leaving the faint scent of her cheap perfume in his nostrils, and he watched her shadowy figure go up the dark street, heels clicking along the sidewalk. 'Youngster wearing scent and high heels already,' he thought vaguely, and waited there in the doorway with the cardboard case in one hand and the feel of sugar on the other.

CHAPTER ELEVEN

In the foyer of the offices of the petroleum company where Isaac worked, a woman with tired, bleached hair and the face of a painted wax doll accidentally left near a fire then hastily retrieved, kept guard in the little telephone exchange behind polished plate glass and mahogany. Behind her, high up on the rear wall of the foyer, a Saudi Arabian king peered down with a slight, amused smile on his bearded face, while the glass-topped table below – for waiting visitors – reflected the curved ornamental dagger in his sash. There was a bowl of flowers on the table and heavy velvet curtains drawn back from the wide window which let in the muted sounds of traffic eight floors below. To left and right of the foyer, past the Arabian king and the tired artificial blonde telephonist, cool, polished parquet corridors with plain, clinical, ultra-modern panelling, ran off into the confines of the company.

Walking along one of the corridors, Isaac prepared himself to be ambushed by the telephonist. She was forever needing something to be done for her: a cream cake from a patisserie – she was careless of her figure – a message to one of the girls in the typing pool, a little more sugar for her tea. The Coloured 'boys' who carried messages for this American firm and served the tea were at her beck and call especially, she seemed to have decided. Everybody, including the entire White staff, considered her a nuisance, but she sat in a tactically advantageous position and few escaped her, particularly the 'boys'.

So, coming along the corridor in his white uniform coat with the name of the company on the breast pocket, Isaac waited for the trap to spring.

'Oh – er – Isaac, will you please get me . . .'

But Isaac scowled at her. 'I have been called to Mister

Goodnight's office, Miss Barrows,' he lied skilfully, mentioning the name of the managing-director of the company. 'Very urgent.'

'Oh, then on your way back,' she persisted wearily. 'Or you could ask one of the other boys. I need some Alka-Seltzer badly.'

'Righto, Miss,' Isaac replied, passing on. Boys, boys, boys, he thought, you could grow to a hundred and they would still call you a boy because you were black. The stupid bitch had been on the tiles again last night; spent all her spare time in hotel bars. He walked on. In actual fact he had been sent to the typing-pool to collect some correspondence for the head of the fuel-oil department. The Harem, he called the typing-pool, although there was little chance of the Saudi Arabian king getting anything from those beautifully preserved hunks of the Master Race. For all the oil he owned, he was still a darkie in this country.

A man came out of an office, pink and smooth as strawberry jelly in his neat grey suit. He carried a file marked 'Bulk Transfers' under his arm and headed blindly past Issac. Mister Bladdy Coames, Isaac said to himself, always thinks he's Jesus Christ Almighty himself, and he's only a second-grade clerk. He reached the door of the typing-pool and opened it.

The chatter of typewriters met him like rifle fire as he entered the big room where rows of elegant, beautifully-kept, mostly young women exuded the mingled scent of perfume, powder and various lotions. Apart from a casual upward glance when the door opened, nobody took any notice of Isaac. The 'boys' were only noticeable when an order had to be given or when a favour was required, otherwise they were part of the furniture, like the grey typewriter covers, the coat rack, the tiny bottles of liquid eraser, copies of memos. Isaac ran the gauntlet of displayed nylon-clad legs, lacquered hair-dos and bright mouths, to the desk that served the fuel-oil department. The girl there did not look up at him: the folder of typed letters lay on a corner of the desk, ready to be taken away. He did not belong to this world of skilled labour and monthly salaries: Black people came into the White-proclaimed city each morning to do the menial work and left each evening to return to the Locations, the Townships, set aside for them like ghettoes. They did not belong with the midday restaurants, the hotels, the apartment houses, the landscaped gardens and the sundrenched beaches on Saturday afternoons, tea on a terrace or cocktails in a plastic and chrome lounge.

A sleekly plump redhead was saying '. . . Can you imagine it? She was actually doing it over a long time, a little bit at a time. It said in the paper this morning that her husband gradually began to feel the effects, like getting sick in the evening.'

'Awful,' said a thin girl with a pale, lean face under layers of eye-shadow and rouge. 'I hear the doctor even told him it might be some kind of polio. Isn't it tea time yet?'

Isaac went out with the folder of letters and when the door had shut, the thin girl looked up. 'Wasn't that the tea boy?' she asked, tapping her teeth with the end of a pencil.

'Speaking of husbands,' the head typist intervened, 'I hear Isobel is getting married at the end of the month. It will mean a collection of course.'

'Isobel in Accounting?' somebody asked.

'It's not right taking a collection if she doesn't invite anybody from down here,' another girl said.

When the chief clerk of the fuel-oil department saw Isaac disappearing through the doorway having left the letters on his desk, he was suddenly reminded of the company's annual outing to the Country Club. The chief clerk was secretary of the staff social club, and he now remembered that he had to ask the 'boys' whether they would help by serving cokes and sandwiches and washing up glasses at the outing, as the Country Club did not supply waiters when it hired out its premises. In the mind of the chief clerk assessments of drums of fuel-oil now became mixed up with quantities of canapes and sandwiches, cases of Coca Cola, beers, and the pairing off of partners for golf. He picked out a pimple on his bald forehead while writing on a memo pad: 'Outing – ask boys to help. Ten shillings for the day.' After all, he thought, they'll probably pinch half the canapes and smoked salmon sandwiches; they're not used to such luxuries. But he decided that he would not ask the one who had just brought in the letters: a surly sort of a bugger, the chief clerk thought. Always on about not being anybody's servant and passing remarks about equality and higher wages, the bloody pop-eyed coon. The other boys knew their place better in the scheme of things. One treated them decently – not like those extremists in the Government – and so one hoped to gain their respect. Last year some of the women objected because they found the 'boys' grinning at them when they appeared in bathing suits at the Country Club's pool. He would have to talk to the 'boys' about that, he thought, fiddling absently with the pimple on his forehead.

When Isaac left the office of the chief clerk of the fuel-oil department, he made his way towards the company kitchen by way of the back corridor, thus avoiding the telephonist in the foyer. In the kitchen the old woman who made the tea was busy setting out cups and saucers on a trolley and bustling around the big water urn that was already boiling. Another messenger in a white jacket sat in a corner at a table, eating sandwiches from a packet, a stack of envelopes of various sizes before him. He smiled and waved a brown hand as Isaac came in.

'*Hoezit, boeta* Ike?' he said. 'What do you say today then?'

'Hullo, Sam,' Isaac said. Then, to the old woman, 'Any chance of getting a cup of tea, ahead of all the Great White Fathers?'

'You got to pour it yourself,' the old woman said, wiping sweat from her fallen chin. 'Is like an oven in here.'

'Blerry warm outside too,' Sam said with his mouth full of polony and bread. 'And I say, my feet are working my case. That old monkey in the mail department give me this whole heap of letters to deliver all over town. When I say to him a lot of the stuff can be posted, you know what he say then? Is cheaper if I deliver then. And my feet so bad, man.'

'You should ask them to get you a scooter,' Isaac said, pouring tea. 'And since you're on the rounds, you better not let *ou* Queen Mother in front catch you, hey. She got a hangover like three sailors and she is crying for Alka-Seltzer, so you might have to leave all the company's business to save her head.'

'I'd like to give her a dose of Epsom Salts,' Sam said. 'Ike, you going to sit in by the *klaberjas* game lunchtime?'

'Hell,' Isaac said, sitting down. 'Is that all you boggers do lunchtime? To play cards?'

'Ah, Ikey, *ou* pal,' Sam said, stirring his tea. 'You could *mos* take us all down the square in the old days to hear a meeting. Nowadays all meetings is *mos* stopped, don't I say? All you can hear now is them holy rollers. There's *mos* nothing else to do. Now we know *mos* you a good *klaberjas* player, pally, and I need a partner.'

'Well, okay then,' Isaac said. '*Klaberjas, klaberjas.*' He grinned at Sam and shook his head. He sat at the table, sipping tea while he doodled with a pencil on a tea-stained sheet of office paper. With his protuding eyes, prominent pink ears, and the permanent look of surprise he wore he was well-liked by most who came in contact with him. He was considered to 'have brains' because he understood many things others in his circle did not, he also 'had nerve' because he challenged every little incident of unfairness or injustice. Now, sitting there in the hot, steamy kitchen, he thought that all this kowtowing to stupid idiots who cherished the idea that they were God's Chosen just because they had white skins, had to come to an end. The silly bastards, he thought, they had been stupefied into supporting a system which had to bust one day and take them all down with it; instead of permanent security and justice, they had chosen to preserve a tyranny that could only feed them temporarily on the crumbs of power and privilege. Now that the writing had started to appear on the wall, they either scrambled to shore it up with blood and bullets and the electric torture apparatus or hid their heads in the sand and pretended that nothing was happening. They would have to pay for stupidity the hard way. Issac felt almost sorry for these people who believed themselves to be the Master Race, to have the monopoly of brains, yet who were vindictive, selfish and cruel.

He woke from his reverie when the door opened and another youth in a white jacket came into the kitchen, asking, 'Tea ready, Missus Williams? The blerry womenfolk are shouting that we five minutes late.'

'Ah, to hell with them,' the old woman said. 'Always complaining, complaining, what do they think? A person's only got two hands. You can take the first trolley.'

'Jump to it,' Isaac told him jokingly. 'When the boss shouts, you got to jump.' He drew a rifle on the soiled sheet of paper before him, while he sipped his tea. As the other youth started to edge the trolley through the door, Isaac added a long magazine and a forward grip to the rifle and turned it into a submachine gun. He said to the one who was pushing the tea-trolley: 'I say, Jannie, if that bloody fool at the telephone ask you where I am, tell her I went out for Goodnight.'

'Is okay, Ike,' the other said. 'I know how it is, hey.'

Jan had the tea-trolley outside now and wheeled it along the corridor. He stopped at each door of the single offices along the corridor and took a cup of tea inside. When he reached the typing-pool he rolled the trolley in and the clattering of type-writers died away like the observance of a cease-fire and newspapers were unfolded, magazines flicked open, cosmetics and hand mirrors dug out of voluminous handbags.

Jannie went around distributing cups of tea and one of the women started reading aloud from the morning newspaper to a typist opposite her: '. . . Putting her hands on the weakened man's chest, she pushed him and he sat down abruptly on the bed. She drew the cord around his neck and started pulling it with both hands, forcing him back to a position sideways on the bed.'

'But couldn't he hit her or something?' the other girl asked, picking up her cup and saucer. 'He *must* have struggled.'

'But he was too *weak*,' another cried. 'The evidence says she was poisoning him little by little.'

'Well, *I* would have struggled.'

'There's something here,' the one who was reading said. 'Oh, yes, it says the accused pulled the cord tighter and her husband's feet began kicking.'

'Ugh, awful,' another voice screamed. 'How *could* she,'

Jannie retreated from the room while murder leaped from one painted mouth to another. He had two more offices to serve from the trolley, and when he was outside in the corridor the elevator doors further down hummed apart and two White men stepped out. They strolled towards the telephonist-receptionist in the glassed-in cubicle under the portrait of the Arabian king.

Both men were tall and redfaced, and one of them was heavy-set while the other was lean and had a long nose and a ginger moustache. The one with the moustache wore flannels and a quiet sports jacket, the heavy one a suit and a felt hat. Seeing them, Jannie felt the old instinct of the slum dweller quickening inside him: he knew that these men had nothing to do with sales of petroleum or the allocation of steel drums to sub-depots. In his mind's eye he saw them behind the long counter on which lay the record of arrests for the day or the night and, coatless, they would reveal the revolvers and automatic pistols in the clip holsters at their waists.

The heavy-set man removed his hat and smiled, nodding at the tired blonde in the cubicle. When he spoke in English it was awkwardly, with a heavy Afrikaans accent. 'Good morning, madam. Can we please see the secretary of the company? I am Sergeant Van Zyl and this is officer Grobbelaar.' He smiled, his mouth like a trap showing white, healthy teeth, his blue eyes like drops of frozen sea water.

Jannie quietly served the last of the cups of tea and when he came out of the office, the two men were out of sight in the foyer while the telephonist was speaking into her head-phone. Jannie had heard the sergeant introduce himself, but before that he had already made up his mind who they were. He went quickly back along the corridor, rolling the trolley ahead, anxious to break the news to those in the kitchen.

He pushed the trolley through the kitchen door and the old woman said, 'What took you so long?'

'I took the usual time,' Jannie said. 'A man can't *mos* handle this thing like it is a bike.' While the old woman set more cups and saucers on the trolley, he said to Sam and Isaac, 'Two law just came in. Spoke to that Miss Barrows. Wonder what they want here. You reckon somebody at the depot's stole some oil or something like that, hey?' He parodied the Sergeant comically: 'Goot morning, hey, I is Sarjent Van Zyl, hey. Has you got a licence?' He laughed and then asked seriously, 'I wonder what those burgs want?'

Isaac had completed a whole array of weaponry, some of it improbable, on the sheet of paper before him. He did not look up at Jannie, but he felt his heart lurch awkwardly inside his chest and the skin of his face crawled and prickled. He became suddenly excited and nervous, but forced the feeling down quickly. Carefully he scored out a weapon which looked like a cross between an old-time blunderbuss and a ray-gun, then put the pencil away in the pocket of his white jacket. He got up and went over to the cupboard in a corner of the kitchen, opened and removed his white company jacket. He took down his own coat and put it on.

Sam looked up and asked, 'Where are you going, Ike? If you wait for me, we can walk together, *mos*.'

'No, I'm in a hurry,' Isaac told him.

'Can you bring me a packet of cigarettes?' the old woman asked, starting to take her purse from her overall pocket.

'I'm going to be away a long time,' Isaac said. 'Sorry.'

He ran a hand over his head and waved to them. 'See you

later then.' He went out of the kitchen thinking that somebody in the group must have talked; it had not come from him. Otherwise how the hell could they know? He went along the corridor and down the back staircase of the building for two floors. Then he walked along another corridor until he reached a doorway that led into the building behind and abutting the block in which he was. He went through this door and past offices let by a dental mechanic, an income-tax consultant and a firm of accountants. Further down the corridor a man in shirtsleeves came out of an office and went towards a door marked 'Gents'. He glanced casually at Isaac before he disappeared into the sound of flushing cisterns. Isaac went on until he reached the front of the building and then went quickly down the staircase next to the lift.

He emerged from the building into the noisy city street, and after the coolness of artificial air-conditioning the heat of the summer day struck him like a blow. The late summer heat danced off the metal of parked cars and lorries, off the surface of the street. For a moment the sunlight blinded him, and he stood with eyes screwed up. When he could focus again, a gang of coloured and African men were unloading crates from a truck parked half a block away, a traffic warden was checking cars parked opposite, and the usual hubbub crawled up and down the throughfare.

He stepped off the sidewalk and crossed the street, dodging the traffic. Nobody shouted after him or tried to impede his progress. He reached the other side with a sense of relief, as if he had eventually arrived safely after passing through miles of enemy territory. The nervousness passed; danger turned nervousness into caution, hesitation into cockiness. He had burned his boats and now there was a feeling of elation inside him that made his step springier.

Far overhead a jet fighter whined, leaving vapour trails in its wake like white scars on the blue skin of the sky. Isaac looked up and watched the plane disappear. They are very strong, he thought. Mirage fighters from France – how long would it take to defeat them? He remembered the national day of protest when he had stood at a window and watched the Saracen armoured cars, troop carriers and trucks advancing along the road towards the Black working-class areas, squat and ugly, like khaki-brown prehistoric insects, armoured and menacing. The patrolling police had been issued with *sjamboks* and had attacked anybody who was not White that they had found on the streets, whipping them mercilessly, because they were automatically presumed to be on strike. Since then Isaac had taken a keen interest in regular and irregular military warfare. He had read history books and the smuggled handbooks on guerilla fighting, he had examined pictures and drawings of small arms of every sort. Theoretically he knew much about Magnums, and about Uzi submachine guns manufactured in Israel. Here, in this country, the principal small arms made locally were the 7.62mm R1 automatic rifles, an improved version of the FN standard NATO rifle and produced under licence from the Fabrique Nationale of Belgium. There were other kinds of guns which could fire a thousand rounds a minute. He knew something about link-belt feeding, 82mm mortars, grenade launchers and bazookas. Corners of his mind were stored with the accumulated knowledge out of technical books and he longed like a lover for the time when he would be able to turn from theory to practice. With his new air of cockiness, the work-a-day jacket and unpressed trousers, the scuffed shoes and the permanent look of surprise, he appeared more like an unsuccessful young man who had just received news of an inheritance than like a potential partisan fighter.

Returning to the present, he realized that somehow he had to let Buke know that he was on the run. The trouble was that it was Beukes who contacted him, not vice versa. Also he had a rendezvous to keep a week from now, which meant he had to hide out somewhere in the meantime. Who the hell had burned him, he asked himself? One of the unit must have been a police plant. Had they arrested other members of the unit?

The security police would have to arrest the nark too, in order to cover up. Nervousness and worry started to creep up on him again, but he thrust it away with a shrug of the youthful shoulders inside the shabby coat.

Isaac walked several blocks and then waited at a bus-stop. When the bus came he climbed to the non-White deck and paid the fare to the furthest point. He sat alone by a window and watched the city unravel past him.

CHAPTER TWELVE

Elias Tekwane sat on the edge of the concrete bunk and stuffed coarse tobacco into the bowl of his pipe. He struck a match and sucked strongly at the stem until the pipe was burning well, and blew clouds of smoke. The smell of the smoke from the cheap tobacco overpowered the other smells in the small, hot cell where he lived with three other men. There were those of sweat, burnt onions, old clothes, and stale cooking, unwashed socks, smoky oil, all intermingled to form one thick, rank, sickly odour which persisted because the single window high up did not open, and more often than not the door was shut all day while the men were away somewhere or other.

On the lower bunk he had to sit crouched forward because the upper one was in the way of his head. Holding his pipe clamped between strong white teeth, he fastened his laced boots, working rapidly with thick, broad-nailed fingers. On the upper bunk opposite him another man slept, snoring heavily, dressed only in soiled shorts, his dark-brown, heavy body gleaming with perspiration, as if he had been painted over with a film of oil. One arm dangled from the bunk and displayed bangles of copper wire on a powerful wrist. He snored steadily and except for the heaving of his chest, his body was limp and motionless.

Elias finished tying his boots and, bare to the waist, got up and went out into the stone corridor to the wash-room at the end of a stone balcony. The wash-room was a cubbyhole with a sink and an evil-smelling toilet with a half-door. He washed briefly at the sink and went back down the corridor to his room, drying himself on a frayed towel.

Along the corridor were similar cells, some of them standing open, and from them came the sounds of life or sleep: a man softly sang a traditional ditty; in one of the rooms a noisy game of dominoes seemed to be in progress; elsewhere a concertina sounded mournfully. It was cooler on the balcony because the summer sun had not reached that part of the barracks yet, but beyond it and below, the Location sprawled in a blaze of cadmium yellow light that quivered and shook with heat, like an old moving-picture.

Back in the room he opened the small tin trunk and found a washed-out khaki shirt and pulled it over his head without removing the pipe from his mouth. The air in the room was hot and thick as flannel. In the free corners the walls were blackened and greasy where the small oil stoves for cooking and heating stood with accompanying battered and blackened saucepans, tin mugs, bent cutlery. Stuffing the tail of the shirt into his trousers, Elias thought, Hauw! You are past forty and still living in a bachelor barracks; you should have a woman. It's against nature and tradition to have no wife. But what difference did a wife make? There were men living in this barracks in the Location who were married and had families, but because their families had not been allowed to come into the city to live with them, they were considered bachelors by the authorities and consigned to these barracks.

Brushing his short, kinky hair while he peered into a scrap of mirror fixed to the door, he tried to remember a girl he had once known, years before.

At that time there were tin shanties everywhere, he thought. Very cold in winter, very hot in summer. The streets had been unpaved and untarred, just a stretch of slum clinging to the edge of the town, like a sore or a boil. Coming back from the town, the smell of rot and stagnant water had been overpowering, but later one had got used to it, to the puddles of dirty water, the mess left by children and animals dotting the pathways like mines in a minefield. Poverty had enveloped the whole scene in a tattered and smelly cloak of rust, decay and destitution. At that time he had known the girl who was not much older than himself. He thought that he must have loved her. Then he had not seen her for many years, he remembered. When he had seen her again, where the tin shacks and the dirty water had been, she had had a baby with a runny nose who was in rags and cried all the time. She was in rags too, but had said that she could not cry any more. The tin shacks had been replaced by rows of brick bunkers: very cold in winter, very hot in summer. What had happened to her, had happened, she had said. No, she did not need any money; the father of the child would bring something sometime, if he ever came home.

That was a long time ago, he thought with a pang of sadness, taking up his old leather jacket with the frayed cuffs. He went out again and shut the door on the sleeping man. You are just over forty and you enjoy what you are doing, in spite of everything, he told himself. According to the pass-book, however, he was almost fifty. His official age had been decided for him by a stupid little clerk the first time he had had to go and take out a pass. They could give you a name and an age, all nicely ready-made, like a hat or a coat out of a shopwindow. Elias could remember the incident very clearly indeed.

The Native Commissioner's Office in his home town was a single-storey building with a rusting metal roof and brown walls. The gutter over the verandah sagged and the rainwater, which poured from it during the wet months, had made a hollow in the areaway in front of it. Behind the dusty front window could be seen a party wall displaying posters issued by the Department of Native Affairs, in three languages, and flyspeckled sheets of paper covered with fine print.

The usual knot of people was gathered below the cracked stoop, but the passes were being issued in the back, through the lopsided motor gate. There was a long table under a shed like an outhouse, officiated over by two White men in shirtsleeves and an African clerk. A Black policeman with a topi and a *knobkerrie* dozed on a bench in the sunlight, apparently ignoring the line of youths and men which had gradually formed up along the back wall of the building. Some of them lounged, others squatted on their haunches, while the clerk called them up one at a time.

'One wastes a whole day here,' one of the men said. 'I want to get a paper to go to the city for the funeral of my brother who has joined the ancestors, but to get it I must lose a whole day. What a stupid thing this is.'

'We are governed by a pack of hyenas,' another man said in reply.

The man who wanted to attend his brother's funeral stuffed a pipe with ragged tobacco, lighted it and puffed small clouds of rank smoke. When the pipe was well alight, he spat into the yard, a thin stream that hissed. He asked the youth who stood two places from him: 'And where are you off to, boy?'

'To the city, uncle,' Elias told him. 'I have just come to get the pass since I am off to work in the big city.'

'You have reached that age then,' the smoking man said. 'How is it with your mother?'

'She is well, but she grows old.'

'So a young boy speaks.' The man with the pipe was about to continue the conversation, but the clerk at the table interrupted, calling to him, and he nodded to the boy, walking away. He wore a disintegrating jacket and shoes soled with pieces of a motor tyre.

Elias and the others sat in the sunshine and waited while the business of the man with the pipe was sorted out. It took a long time. The sun moved across the yard, pushing the shadow of the building ahead of it. Elias sat sleepily in the sun and tried to recapture the adventures of the men in his book. They had all been good warriors and had fought in battles with foreign names. The blood stirred in him in spite of the torpor, and his mind switched to the tales told by the old people of the village, of the battles fought by their ancestors. To be a warrior like them, he thought; to fight these people who lived in this country yet behaved like foreigners, like jackals and birds of prey, persecuting the bodies of old women still living. He saw the raised *assegais,* the hide shields like great pods, and heard the stamp of feet and the ululation of the women, and he saw men like that Wasserman who had called him a black thing, a baboon, fleeing before him. He wanted to shout after Wasserman, but somebody else was crying, 'Hey, are you asleep?'

Elias recalled how he had sprung to his feet and had marched towards the table, his sturdy body defiant. Behind the portable table on trestles under the outhouse, the two White clerks worked at sheaves of papers and ignored Elias as he came up. Now he felt a little apprehensive and not certain of whom to address, so he stood hesitantly before the table, waiting.

The African clerk, who wore red braces, said in a bored voice: 'Well, big boy, so it is time to become a man, is it not?'

'A man?' asked Elias, frowning.

'*Yebo,*' Red-braces said in the same bored tone. 'Now you will become part of what the White people have done for this land. The big bosses have ordained that only when you carry the pass will you be a man.' There was a hint of sourness under the bored voice, and his eyes, purple-spotted, were cynical. He leaned back in his folding chair and ran thick thumbs, like scorched sausages, up and down behind the red braces and snapped them against his chest.

'Man, you talk too much,' one of the White officials said, looking up. 'Get on with the job, *jong.*'

Red-braces grinned at Elias and drew forward a printed form. Elias stood there and looked at this man. He shifted on his feet and somewhere in the back of his mind there formed the idea that this man, with his bored expression and tobacco-stained grin, was teasing him, not in a friendly way, but in the way a cat teases a mouse – a jocular cuff and a delicate nudge, each playful blow jovially bringing death nearer.

Red-braces took up a pencil and tapped the end of it against his teeth. One of the officials stopped his work in order to light a cigarette, then resumed his writing.

Red-braces said abruptly: 'Let me see your paper stating where you will work. Ah. Your name then?'

Elias had told him.

'What is the name of your father?'

'He is dead.'

'Boy, I did not ask whether he was alive or dead. I asked for his name.'

Elias told him.

'What is the name of your mother? What is the name of your Chief?'

'Chief? I did not think I would be asked his name, since he lives far in another part.'

'You are a fool,' Red-braces said. 'A fool. I can see great trouble ahead for you. What is the name of your headman? There is a headman in the village, is there not?'

Red-braces filled in the particulars with a scratchy pen. He asked: 'How many years do you have?'

'Seventeen,' Elias told him. All these questions fretted him. He wondered why these people should want to know all these things. One had a name and parents and ancestors; those were enough.

The clerk said sceptically: 'Do not play with me. Seventeen years? With a beard and all?'

The second official had looked up from his work and asked, 'What is it with this one?'

'His age, boss,' Red-braces said, turning his head to look at the White man. 'He says he is only seventeen.'

The second official said, 'He's a *skelm*, a cheat. They are all liars, these. He is too big for seventeen.'

'That is what I say, too,' Red-braces said deferentially. He appeared pleased that his superior agreed with him.

The first official said, 'God, it's easy to find out.' He looked across the boards at Elias. 'You, take down your pants, *jong*.'

Elias looked back at him, startled and puzzled. He was not sure he had heard this White man correctly. The official looked impatient this time and said sharply, 'Hey, did you not hear me, you? I said let your —— pants down.'

Elias looked now at Red-braces, feeling the blood rush to his face. The Black clerk laughed as he said, 'Do as the *baas* says, big man. Let us see you.' He gestured at his waistband. 'The trousers. Take off the trousers.'

Bewildered, Elias plucked at his shabby trousers and worked them down over his hips and thighs. He did not look at Red-braces and did not undo the buttons, hoping that the omission would compensate for embarrassment. He held the trousers sullenly below his hips. Red-braces leaned over and, grinning, lifted Elias's shirt with the end of his pen.

Then he laughed and said to the officials: 'He has gone through the rites already, but he has a beard there too. He is never seventeen. I would say the scoundrel is no less than twenty.'

The first official said, 'He has taken the girls out into the bushes too, I bet you. Write twenty.'

'Right, boss,' Red-braces said. To Elias, 'You fasten up the trousers. We do not need to see it any longer.'

Elias said, drawing up his trousers and feeling shamed: 'I am seventeen, seventeen, seventeen.'

'Twenty,' Red-braces said. 'The boss has said you are twenty, and twenty years you are.' He smiled triumphantly at Elias and wrote on the form. Elias looked at his dusty toes, feeling his face hot with shame and the stab of anger in his chest.

Afterwards he was motioned through the door into the Commissioner's office where other ragged men waited on a bench before a counter. He set down at the end of the line and then all waited in silence, while he nursed the flame of rage within him. Time limped across the wall of the room, across the notices, the rusty thumbtacks. Then a door opened behind the counter and a fat, redfaced man came out. He wore a tight waistcoat and a rigid gold watch-chain across the paunch, as if he needed to prevent his insides from dropping

127

out. He looked over his spectacles at the men who stood up, shuffling.

'You, put out that *verdomte* thing,' he snapped at the man who was puffing at his long pipe. 'This is not a bloody *kaffir kraal*.'

He looked at the sheaf of forms he held in a ruddy hand, and proceeded to read out names.

So they made me older than I really am, Elias thought, and smiled to himself. They have command of everything now, even the length of time one is entitled to lived in this world. If they do not do it with the gun or the hangman's rope, they can easily write it out on a piece of paper, ending days, years, life, like a magician he had once seen at a concert, making playing-cards disappear.

Coming out of the barracks into the hard glare of the sunlight in the Location, carrying his coat over one shoulder, he made his way towards the distant beer-hall.

In the sandy square, fat women sat behind boards laid on petrol drums, displaying the heaps of offal for sale – they fetched it from the local abbatoirs. Sheep's heads, bundles of tripe, pink piles of liver curling like plastic in the sun, while the fat hands drove away the squadrons of flies swooping down. Corn-on-the-cob roasted in four-gallon cans on braziers, and the smoke rose in straight columns as from sacrificial offerings. On a sidewalk the barbers were busy with customers who sat in a row shirtless and perspiring, and the scissors went snick-snick, winking dully in the razor-sharp sunlight.

Beyond all this the rows of family houses, squat cubes mostly, stretched away like battalions of pillboxes. In front of some of them picket fences and sandy gardens struggled to make a show of colour, like faded bunting hung out to decorate a chicken farm. Behind a maze of wire fences lay the administration centre: the Police Station with the flag of the Republic hanging limp above it, an armoured land-rover, and two convicts in red blouses and white canvas shorts weeding the lawn; the Bantu Commissioner's office; the labour bureau where a restless crowd assembled around a White official who called out vacancies from a chair on which he stood. 'Messenger boy, sweeper, builder's labourer ...'

At the entrance to the beer-hall, the usual municipal policeman with a club sat on a bench and squinted in the sunlight. There had been a riot at the hall one night and since then the City Council had posted a man on guard. From inside the long building came the buzz of voices and through the smudged windows Elias could see a few men sitting at the long table under the ribbons of fly paper.

At the rear exit, near the public lavatory, was a telephone booth, its windows empty of glass, the floor littered, as if it had survived a bomb blast. Elias discovered with relief that the wires were still intact. Usually the instrument was ripped out by the Location vandals – was it a form of protest against authority, he wondered?

He stood in the exposed cubicle and felt for a five-cent piece, he dialled and waited while the phone rang at the other end. Across the strip of street a potbellied child in a ragged shirt made water into the dust. The telephone clicked and a voice said, 'Hullo? Purity Pharmacy here,' and Elias slipped the coin in, relieved again that it did not stick in the slot.

He said, 'Can I speak to Mister Polsky, please?' He waited again, while the pharmacist was being called. The heat haze danced and quivered above the roofs of the Location. Then, 'Polsky here.'

'Mister Polsky, hullo, this Mister Hazel speaking here.'

'Oh, hello, Hazel. How are you keeping today?'

'I'm well, yes. Did my friend collect the medicine I ordered?'

'Oh, yes, he came for the medicine. It was handed over to your man.'

'Ah, then thank you Mister Polsky.'

'All right. I hope the medicine helps you, sir.'

'I think it will do some good, yes. Well, goodbye then.'

He hung up and took his coat from the door handle where

he had left it, and went out of the booth. Going towards another part of the Location, he thought that Beukes must have got his material. Beukes would see that the stuff went out, he was reliable, and he had a unit functioning. This section was a little shaky, but up to now they had worked quite well and had not been uncovered. The organization was somewhat lopsided, some sections having very good facilities and equipment, others having to do the best they could.

Beukes was all right, Elias thought. He was something of a flag-waver, but he understood and was sincere. So far they had not caught up with him and that was most important. Who could tell how anybody would react in the hands of the Security Police; every man had his limit. In his mind's eye he saw a comrade falling seven floors from the police headquarters, to his death on the concrete below. What had they done to him?

Beukes had been in the movement for some time. Elias remembered the first time he had met Beukes. It had been at a committee meeting in connection with a campaign against the mass removals of people. When the deadline came, the police would surround an area, a 'Black spot' in the White zone and load everybody onto a convoy of trucks. Hours later they would arrive in the place the Government had marked out for them on a map, and there they would be unloaded: the battered furniture, hastily-packed suitcases and boxes, the children wailing in the open veld. They were 'home'. Perhaps a long time afterwards there would be a settlement of shanties and gim-crack dwellings, or the authorities would come along and build the usual bunkers themselves. The people were not going to be moved without making a protest and they had called for support. Elias remembered Beukes then, a young man with a small scar which gave relief to the delicate cast of his face. From then onward they had worked well together when circumstances demanded.

When the movement had gone underground, Elias had wondered who would stick, take the risks, and when word had come down that he should set up a section in a certain part, Elias had sent out feelers carefully, like a doctor probing for a shell-splinter in a dangerous place. He had felt pleasure when he had discovered Beukes emerging.

At the meeting he had said, 'Well, I am very glad to see you with us again.' As they spoke, he had said: 'Our rulers are trying hard to create divisions among us. We are each supposed to have our own this and our own that. Even a sort of democracy, our own councils which we shall elect ourselves, under *their* supervision.'

Beukes had added: 'In the same way the Nazis allowed councils for Jews in the ghettoes, while assisting them to the gas ovens. There is even talk that we should be allowed to use their new opera house. But it is difficult to go to a posh theatre if you are poor and live miles away in a segregated slum.'

Elias had chuckled. 'What a peculiar way of thinking they have,' he had said. 'Opera house and no bread.' There had been something about the copper-brown eyes and the smile with the long upper lip which had inspired confidence, which had given assurance of a sort of faith

But these days one could not depend only on faith: the apparatus of the Security Police scraped away faith and perseverence like strata of soil until they came to what was below. If they reached crumbly sandstone, it was splendid for them. It was the hard granite on which they foundered. You are worrying too much, Elias told himself. How do you know what is below? It is no use speculating. He hoped that everybody would do what he had to and would behave in the correct way when the test came. If we worried how tough each man was, we would get nowhere. It is the Security Police who set the examinations.

He passed the administration block again. The convict gardeners had disappeared, but there was still a crowd around the labour bureau, waiting for the menial jobs. Walking past, he thought we are not only humbled as Blacks, but also as workers; our blackness is only a pretext. He recalled coming to the city for the first time as a youth (or as a man, according to the age they had put on his pass). He had worked at a laundry for two pounds and ten shillings a week. From that he had had to pay the rent in the old Location where they had sent him, as well as the taxes, and feed himself and save in order to send something home to his mother. He had saved some money and three winters later he had gained permission to visit his village in the country.

He recalled his trip home to the countryside that winter; it was then that he had seen the miner who had come home from the mines carrying pthisis. It was strange that he should have found the sight of the miner more moving than the meeting with his old mother again. He had been thin and bent and had coughed all the time. He had brought no sweets for the children, as Elias had managed to do. In fact, the children had been afraid of him; he was so quiet, moved so slowly, his eyes very big and bloodshot. The children had said that he had been bewitched because he had stolen something from somebody. But Elias knew he had been a miner and wondered whether his own father would have come home like that after having spent himself digging up gold. Perhaps it was better that he had died suddenly down there, far below.

Elias saw too that the open air of the countryside, the stillness and the songs of the birds also hid the destitution. The food from the fields was beginning to run out, then would come the collection of weeds, if the weather had not yet dried them up: they would also serve for food. Then came the interminable debts with the White shopkeeper. There was ignorance in the countryside too; in that part of the land one did not see any meetings like the ones which were held in the city. In the cities it was not easy to avoid the movement. The people stirred under the weight of tyranny, then went to meetings in the squares, halls, houses, to listen to the speakers.

Elias had not returned to the countryside after that. He felt that the brown, eroded land, the little dwellings on the scrubby hillside held little for him. Besides, his blood had dripped onto the hard grey surface of a city sidewalk, and it was as if it had taken root and held him there. The laundry workers had gone on strike for better wages and he had gone to a meeting oustide the big washing plant. *Umanyano*, the union, was not recognizcd, of course, and strikes by Africans were illegal: they were, according to law, not workers, but servants, and the contract bound them fast. The management had sent for the police and they had charged the strikers with truncheons.

Elias recalled the warmth of the pavement against his face and the smell of dust as he lay there. Around him feet ran before the swinging clubs. His head ached and there was an additional sharp pain across his scalp where the club had caught him; he could feel the blood, like warm syrup, trickling slowly down the side of his face and forming a pool on the paving. He had been afraid; his heart thumped and his mouth was dry, and he had thought, why, why why?

On another day a grubby letter had arrived, passed from hand to hand, telling him that his mother had died more than a month before. All his links with the countryside had then been broken. He had wept a little at the news, knowing that now, more than ever, he had to be truly a man.

Suddenly, as he walked through the Location in the hot, yellow, dancing sunlight, he smiled, remembering his fear, and told himself, 'You have come a long way since then, man, and how far will you still go?'

CHAPTER THIRTEEN

On the dim staircase the air was heavy with the old odours of broken lavatories and dustbins, all mingled to form a fetor not unassociated with exhumed graves. Night had not cooled the atmosphere inside the grimy building and Beukes climbed into the gloom and the smell like a grave-robber who had just broken into a tomb. Behind the anonymous doors poverty had retreated into unpeaceful sleep, and the hallway to Tommy's was deserted except for a dried trail of tea-leaves and curling scraps of paper. The floorboards cracked and snapped underfoot as he made his way tiredly towards Tommy's room, like a weary swimmer breasting the sea.

He found the key above the door where he had left it, and he thought with tired humour, not home yet; that ballroom committee must be having an all-night sitting. The electric lamp revealed the big radiogram again, the stacked records, the picture of the band-leader. He had not shut the window when he had left, so the air was relatively clear in the room, and the faint night breeze stirred the curtains faintly, like the hand of a ghost. Beukes shut the door behind him and dropped the cardboard case on a chair as he plodded towards the untidy bed. He sat on the bed and yawned, dragging his shoes off with relief. He sat there, wiggling his toes and feeling contentment as his feet found comfort.

He found his cigarettes and lighted one. Sitting on the bed, smoking, too weary to get undressed he thought, can't even use that taxi for a job like this because the driver would then know each area and address. He wondered about Isaac. Where the hell was Isaac? Had any of his people been picked up?

He started as the neglected cigarette burned his finger and he crushed it out on the floor. After that he stripped tiredly to his underwear, went to turn out the light, and crawled into the untidy bed.

In the dark he saw Frances and their child. He was glad there was a child, in spite of everything. He remembered the fearful dreams he had had while Frances had been pregnant. He had dreamed of Frances pregnant and shot in the belly, or with her abdomen torn open by wild dogs, bayonets, spears: Frances writhing in pain and blood and horror.

The dreams had come after that time when that other woman had been shot. There had been a big meeting to protest against the rise in bus fares: the people could not afford higher transport costs to and from their Townships and Locations far outside the city. It had been quite a big meeting, and then right in the middle of it all the police had barged in to arrest a single drunk who had fallen asleep. It had been an obvious and arrogant provocation, and the people, tempers already aroused, had tried to rescue the drunken man They had marched on the local police station. The police had opened fire: four men had been shot in the arm, mouth, neck and back; a fifteen-year-old girl had been shot in the chest. The pregnant woman had been shot in the stomach.

After that had come the dreams. He remembered waking in the night, shivering, and Frances's voice beside him, caught between anxiety and surprise. 'What is it, dear? What's the matter, man? A bad dream?' After several such nights, Frances, big with child, had said seriously, 'Maybe you should go and see a doctor. You could get something to make you sleep.' He had not told her about the dreams, and he had been glad and happy when the child had been born all right.

Now he still dreamed about Frances and their daughter, but not with such horror. He dreamed of Frances falling through space, Frances falling from a high tower, falling, falling, falling, with no-one to catch her. Sometimes he would be falling with her. But those dreams were not as bad as the others had been, although he still woke up with a feeling of fear.

One evening he had come home after talking with Elias; Frances had not been in and the baby's cot was empty. He had hung his coat in the wardrobe and had gone to the kitchen to sit by the stove and read the evening newspaper until Frances returned. When she arrived she had had the child on her arm and had said, 'There's daddy.' He had taken the child from her and she had kissed him on the cheek. 'Say hullo to daddy,' she had smiled. 'Sorry I wasn't here when you came, but Missus Roberts got something wrong with her. Pains. I think it's some kind of colic, but the doctor didn't turn up so I went down to see what I could do. My brother used to get it. The food's in the oven so I'll put the baby in the cot and then dish up.'

'Is our baby okay?' Beukes had asked, nuzzling the child's cheek.

'Oh, she's been sleeping well. No trouble with her. She's a good girl, good, good, good.'

Beukes had sat at the kitchen table with his thoughts while Frances had gone to attend the child to bed. After she had come back to the kitchen and was setting the table for the supper, he had still been quiet, frowning.

Frances had said, 'I gave her a bottle. Is something wrong?'

They had sat opposite each other with the plates of cabbage stew between them and Beukes had gazed at her across the table. He had said, 'Well, it's nothing that's *wrong* actually.'

'Well, you better tell me now '

'It's that they want me to do this work. It will mean that I got to leave home.'

'No, man, not that. Not for good, hey?'

'Well, not necessarily. Maybe only for a while at a time. You see, I'm one of the few the police don't know about. I don't reckon so, anyway.'

'Do you want to do it?'

He had said desperately: 'I don't *have* to. But, well, there's so few, so damn few now to do the work. With all those people in prison we got to almost start all over again. We've got to keep it alive, see?'

Frances had said humbly, 'Oh, man, I don't want you to leave me, us.' Then smiling a little. 'Well, if they asked you, they must trust you a lot. I'm proud of you. Your aunt brought you up well.'

He had asked, 'What about you? And the baby?'

'Well, I still got my job at the faktry, and I can stay with my ma week-ends She'll love to have us there, especially her granddaughter. When you go you see that you take proper clothes, your sweater and pyjamas. When will you go?'

He had giggled a little hysterically: 'Pyjamas. Francy, you think of the funniest things, hey.' Then he had asked, 'What will your old man say? That I can't look after his daughter?'

'Ach, you leave my pa and ma to me. Now you better eat up, and we can talk some more later on.'

She had come over to kiss him and her mouth had tasted of cabbage. I'm lucky, he had thought. There must be other women like her but I'm lucky to have her, just her, just this one. It was a real lucky thing I went to that fun-fair, but you didn't win her at no coconut-shy, man. Not at any coconut-shy.

Now, trying to fall asleep in the stale, hot and soiled bed, his mind drifted like a leaf tossed here and there on the surface of a pond. Nelly Bennett, he remembered, damn bitch. He recalled Arthur Bennett, nervous, harrassed, ashamed, small and bald, his eyes pleading. Poor old Arty had always been nervous, even in those days before the movement had been outlawed.

Legality had been no guarantee and you had had to be careful then too. And the very necessity for care and vigilance had estranged Bennett. His nagging wife had also undermined his shaky enthusiasm, like a tide washing away sandy foundations.

'It's not that I don't *want* to go on,' Bennett had said, 'but a man's got to consider things. The cops are busy. All known people are being pulled in for questioning, I hear. The bloody Minister got powers to deal with people as he likes. A man's got to consider: there's a job and the house and – and Nelly. She's not bad, Buke, really, but she keeps on so. You know how it is, hey?'

'No, I don't, man,' Beukes had told him, feeling cruel.

'Well, maybe Frances isn't like Nelly. I don't know. But a man got to consider.'

They were driving to a place where Beukes had to attend a special meeting of a joint committee. The place was out of the way and he had got Bennett to drive him there in his old pick-up truck. They had driven bouncily through the lamplit streets, Bennett peering nervously through the stained windscreen. It was raining and the rain beat like hands against the windows. Beyond the cabin of the truck, the world – buildings, the few people out, all grey and gloomy, drained of colour – was locked in the sheeting rain.

Then, feeling contrite at having spoken harshly, he had said, 'Never mind, I understand. You don't have to worry, man. Each of us, we do what we can, isn't it?' And he thought, who am I to judge him? How long will I last in this?

'I'll wait for you,' Bennett had said, a little sheepishly. 'It's raining bad.' They had arrived at the place of the meeting.

'What about your wife?' Beukes had asked. 'She'll want to know where you've been all night.'

'Oh, I'll tell her something,' Bennett had replied. 'I'll think of something to tell her.'

That had also been the first time that Beukes had met Elias Tekwane whose code name was now Hazel.

'We're glad you could come,' Elias had said. He was sitting at the head of the table in the room with the decorated lampshade and the bright curtains. The owners of the house had gone out for the night and Beukes had not known to whom the house belonged. They had shaken hands all round, all the people in the room.

'I think this committee is representative of this region,' Elias had begun. 'If we have people from all sections of the population, we should make this campaign a success.' The light had picked out his face, broad and dark-brown, the eyes under the heavy brows were flecked; he had an untrimmed moustache and a scanty, crisp beard surrounded the wide, heavy mouth. He had smiled with large teeth while from an old leather jacket came the smell of tobacco. He had a thick, clumsy, cheerful voice, and he chose all his words carefully as if he had to think of each in turn as he spoke in English, fiddling with a pencil held in big, rough fingers.

Outside, the rain had drummed down and they had sat around the table in the silent house with the raincoats dripping behind the door, talking quietly.

Later Elias had said, 'Man, it is becoming quite clear that the Government will not allow the people to organize as before. Yes, they cannot proceed with their plans while allowing the people to prepare to resist. So they will have to outlaw us. Our problem, friends, is going to be that we will have very few people not already known to the police. Mass activity has meant that we have had to expose our cadres. It cannot be helped, because by activity the people's understanding develops. But those of us not yet known, should work with great caution.'

The meeting had proceeded and afterwards they had shaken hands again and had left, one by one. Beukes had been the last one to leave, and before he went out Elias had said to him, 'Comrade, things can become very bad. Are you worried?'

Beukes had smiled at him, 'I reckon we all worry.'

'I mean about yourself,' Elias had said. 'Not about what we have to do, but about you, yourself.'

Beukes had felt that for some reason this man was now testing him, and he had said, 'Perhaps you are worried too. That is why you ask about me. You reckon to yourself, I wonder if he can be trusted? One day they might get hold of him and then he will name me. Hey?'

Elias had chuckled in his thick voice. 'Maybe you are right.' They had shaken hands again and he had gone out in his damp raincoat. The rain had stopped and the street glistened in the tired pallor of the lamplight. He had walked around the block, the cold thrusting like a sword through his damp clothes, to where Bennett waited in his little pick-up. Bennett had fallen asleep in the corner of the cabin, the pallid light on his bald forehead, his mouth open, and Beukes had thumped on the window until he had woken up. It was past midnight and they had driven back through the chill, sleeping city that shone like polished gun-metal in the darkness. He wondered what excuse Bennett had made to his wife that night.

CHAPTER FOURTEEN

A slum hung on the edge of the city suburbs like dirty plaster, cracking and crumbling away, yet unwilling to fall apart. There were ruined and broken lines of gimcrack cottages where the main suburb ended and then winding and broken lines of dwellings with rusting walls and sagging roofs held down with stones or baling wire. In the late-summer night the darkness slowly edged away the dry sand-lots, the rutted lanes that passed for streets, the sagging fences that surrounded arid patches which were hopefully used as gardens, and left only the dim lights like smudged gold tinsel scattered haphazardly against a shabby cloth of smoky purple. It was the frontier between the official 'Bantu' Township that sprawled behind wire fences, the Coloured and Asiatic zones, and the White-proclaimed city. One day the ragged settlement of cardboard, flattened metal drums and tottering cottages, would disappear, its habitants neatly packed off into various categories like specimens in a museum, but now it hung on, in unconscious defiance of what was euphemistically termed 'slum clearance'.

From the window of the room in which they met, Beukes could see the shadowy outline of shanties strung carelessly together, a withered tree, a fence of bare branch-poles. Somewhere a dog barked and another gave answer. He settled the curtain over the window while the mosquitoes tapped the panes, and went back to the table where Elias sat. A large oil lamp burned on it and its light flickered nervously around the the walls which had been papered with sheets of rejected advertising material from a printers; parts of lithographed pictures and lettering overlapped without order; a dismembered hand emerged from a label for plum jam, and a mouth smiled under a speedboat. It was like being in a small gallery

141

devoted to surrealistic art. Otherwise, there was a picture of an African vocal group and a shelf containing a bible, and old school readers. The room smelled of paraffin from the lamp. The wick needs trimming, Beukes thought idly, while the floor sagged under his feet. He wondered who lived here, but he knew he should not ask. The mosquitoes tap-tapped against the window.

From the table where he sat Elias said, grinning with large teeth: 'It is okay. There is somebody on watch outside as usual. And we will not be long.'

Beukes sat down in the chair opposite him; they might have been preparing to tell each other's fortune – even the decor seemed appropriate. But there were no teacups, no cards on the table, only the newspapers which Elias had brought, and the lamp. Elias turned the wick up and the brighter light made his shadow loom up on the surrealistic walls, like a crouched bull. The glass chimney smoked and the smell of paraffin was stronger, so he trimmed the flame down again. His shadow, jerking in the light, contracted from the strips of labels, the dissected pictures and the lithographed words.

Elias brought out his pipe and stuffed it with tobacco. Striking a match he said, sucking at the mouthpiece, 'We have to discuss defects in our organization in the section. But, before anything else, if there is an alarm, man, you go at once through the back and run like hell, yes. That is the best we can arrange. You understand?'

'I know,' Beukes said. 'We've been over it before.' He took out his own cigarettes and lighted one. A disembodied eye on the wall stared at him cynically over the other man's shoulder.

'Are you nervous?' Elias asked, smiling.

'Hey, nervous as a bugger,' Beukes confessed, smiling back wrily with his long upper lip, his eyes like moist copper. 'But should we have met so soon after? But then, I reckon I will never get used to this.' Elias's mention of an alarm had made his stomach cold.

142

'None of us gets used to it, boy,' Elias said. 'All the time we have to take the chance. But just remember, right out the back and run, run, run. The place is like a jigsaw puzzle so they can't cover everywhere.'

Beukes shook his head as if he was shedding water. 'Let's get on with business.' He wanted to get it over and then get out of the place. The smoky fumes from the lamp hurt his eyes.

Elias nodded seriously then and went on. 'First, I was to tell you that there are three men who have to be taken north and across the border. They are going to be trained for the military wing. Since you are in charge of transport for the first stage of the trip from here, you should arrange for your man to take them. They will meet on Monday at the usual place for such things.'

'Will I know them?' Beukes asked.

'I don't know,' Elias answered, puffing at his pipe. 'But they will be named Peter, Paul and Michael.' He laughed through the drifting grey smoke. 'We are making use of the saints. Perhaps I should not be Hazel. There is no Saint Hazel, is there?'

'Not that I ever heard of,' Beukes smiled. 'Saint Hazel, hey? If there were four of us we could be Matthew, Mark, Luke and John.' Somewhere out in the dark the dog yapped again and the siren of a train wailed distantly.

'Well,' Elias said. 'Michael, Peter and Paul then, and you will see that they get away all right, yes?'

'Of course,' Beukes said and dropped the end of his cigarette in a saucer which served as an ashtray. The lamp flickered faultily and he looked at it for a moment. He said, 'It is a good thing that we are now working for armed struggle. It gives people confidence to think that soon they might combine mass activity with military force. One does not like facing the fascist guns like sheep.' It was like a slogan.

'Well, we have started,' Elias said, 'We are beginning to recover from earlier setbacks. Step by step our people must acquire both the techniques of war and the means for fighting such a war. It is not only the advanced ones, but the entire people that must be prepared, convinced.' He sucked at his pipe and the smell of tobacco deadened the paraffin fumes. 'Anyway, on Monday they must be off, Peter, Paul and Michael.' He tapped the newspapers which he had unfolded on the table. 'Here is part of our work to convince the people. You have seen the news, yes?'

'Made a point of it first thing,' Beukes said.

He had awakened early that morning after a sweltering night in Tommy's bed. The first light of day had been creeping in, tinged wth the grey of approaching autumn, and was shifting the shadows out of the room, off the wardrobe, the radiogram, the wash basin. Tommy had slept beside him in the wooden double bed, invisible under a blanket in spite of the heat. From beyond the window and the old balcony outside, across the flattened building sites, had come the far-away voice of a *muezzin* calling the faithful to prayer: the only mosque left in the bulldozed district, it stood there, making a last ditch stand against the encroaching Infidel. Beukes had wakened Tommy who had later gone to buy the first editions. But there had been nothing in the early papers and he had waited impatiently, like a ticket-holder anxious to hear the results of a lottery, for the next papers.

Elias said, 'From the reports it looks as if everything went very well. Hauw! we have them puzzled, I think. Look, in some places they used most up-to-date methods: explosive devices they call them, and even a broadcast with tape recorders.' He added, as if apologising for their own simple methods, 'The distribution by hand went quite well too.'

Beukes had already read the reports with some astonishment. The headlines splashed in black, astounded letters: 'Explosions scatter pamphlets ... Leaflet bombs hit the city ... Underground movement still active.' The woman who had murdered her husband had been relegated to an inside page. 'The Minister of Police made the observation that the leaflet explossions were an indication that undermining elements were still active. The public must not think that the dangers are a thing of the past . . .' A picture showed two uniformed police looking down at parts of a leaflet bomb. A report from another city stated that crowds going to work that morning had suddenly been harangued by speeches broadcast from tape-recorders left with timing devices in abandoned cars. Other items said that leaflets from the illegal underground movement had been found in letterboxes, under doors and in pathways in various parts. A headline announced italically: 'Security Police promise widespread investigations.'

'One of my people has disappeared,' Beukes said, taking out his handkerchief and wiping his eyes that burned from the fumes from the lamp.

Elias looked up from the newspapers. 'As a result of this?'

'No. It was before I could get to him with the leaflets. I think it was that they just happened to find out about him.'

'He got away?'

'Yes, but where, I don't know.'

'Too bad,' Elias said. 'But at least they did not get him. We are a little loose here in this section, hey? Our contacts, lines of communication. It is something we will have to talk about. The trouble is that we do not have many people doing this work professionally as yet. They live at home. In order to remedy this . . .'

Something rattled on the roof of the house, a stone flung, bouncing across corrugations. Elias was on his feet and turning down the lamp. Beukes could see his teeth through the short, scrubby beard, white in the broad, dark-brown face. He was on his feet too, looking surprised. The light went out, the fantasy disappeared from the walls like the end of a film, and Elias's voice snapped heavily: 'Run, man. Go.'

Beukes blundered in the dark, knocking over his chair as he headed in the direction of the door in the rear of the little room. He barged through a kitchen, the outlines of metal sauccpans and an iron stove in a fireplace crossed his vision while he went through to the back door of the house. His stomach was tight and cold inside him, like the stab of an icicle, and his heart lurched on broken springs.

In the dark yard a flashlight blazed suddenly over a fence and he swerved aside while a voice, gutteral and comanding, shouted at him. He crashed into another fence of rickety poles, feeling it give under his weight. He fell through, scattering flimsy wood. There were lights coming on from cars all over the area behind him, and he smashed through a barrier of rubbish; wheels, boxes, cans toppling about him in a clamour of falling junk. His mind said, run, run, run, and he skidded in the dust of a sandy alleyway. He was aware of several voices, ordering, shouting. He was somewhere away from the house, but pain jabbed his arm with the searing burn of white-hot iron and he stumbled, falling to his knees, while the sound like snapping wood came to him from somewhere a distance behind.

He scrambled back to his feet, clawing at the arm that hurt and burned, and he thought raggedly, 'oh, God, oh my God. My arm. My arm.'

He was in a dark alleyway flanked by jerry-built shanties and broken-down cottages. A dog on a chain hurtled at him through a fence, snapping and fighting against the chain that held it back. Somewhere doors were opening, slamming, voices enquiring shrilly. He went up the alleyway, holding onto his arm, and the palm and the back of his hand were sticky and warm. From the darkness came the stench of exposed lavatories, but he felt only pain. He muttered, panting like a broken kettle, 'Jesus, I must have been shot.' For a moment he thought, with shock and terror, that he was about to die, but then realized that it was his arm and not any vital part of his body which had been wounded. For a while he ran, his legs shaky and his knees painful, while his breath came in great gulps. He ran on until exhaustion overcame him and he sat down by a dark fence, not caring any more whether they caught him or not.

After a while he realized that his arm hurt badly and he held the bloody sleeve of his coat tightly. He was shivering, as if he had been out in the rain and had caught a chill. He drew up his knees and lay his head upon them in the dark, and moaned and panted with shock, in a state of breathless fear, like a man trapped in a mine. Around him the summer night was quiet.

Some time passed and then he lifted his head. His mouth was dry and he was feeling hollow. Overhead, the star-pearled sky was hazy with faint wisps of fog. He could see the dark walls of suburban houses. His arm hurt and the hollowness persisted. From somewhere came the hoot of a motor-horn, a mysterious, inexplicable sound heard by a man newly landed on an apparently empty planet.

He sat there in the dark for a long time. He experienced a brief spell of exhilaration and thought, giggling hysterically, I'm shot. I've been shot, hey. The cops uncovered the house and the —— look-out fell down on the job, and I've been shot. Dammit, it's like a bladdy Western movie. Then his head spun, his stomach started to turn and he leaned over in time, wincing as he moved the wounded arm, and vomited on the ground beside him. His head whirled and the feeling of nausea remained; he lay his head on his knees again and felt the world rise and fall with him. Like being on a ferris wheel, he thought. Why was he thinking of a ferris wheel?

Later he climbed to his feet. You must get far away, he ordered himself. His knees felt wobbly. You've got to walk, walk, walk. There was nobody about. The darkness held warmth, but he plodded wearily into it, like somebody facing a gale. He thought, through the pain in his arm, I want to go home, I must go home, I want to go home to Francy. He still felt hollow but it was not the hollowness of hunger, and he realized, with tears pricking his eyeballs, that it was the hollowness of abandonment.

Pain focused attention on his wounded arm. He realized that it had stopped bleeding, but that the sleeve of his coat was soggy with blood. Lord, he thought, that's my blood, my own blood. The arm pained and burned. I need a doctor, he told himself anxiously. The only doctor he might be able to trust lived miles away in another part of the world, another part of the universe.

Sometime later, he looked about and discovered that he had wandered into some upper-class White suburb. Tall gates, high walls, dark hedges bordered the street. The streetlamps cast a bluish, oily glow along the thoroughfare. Beyond massed greenery dance music sounded distantly, and ahead of him he saw a wooden bench in a recess in a neatly-clipped hedge: elderly ladies out for walks could rest there or the nursemaid could stop to air the baby.

He made his way over to the bench. From behind the tall hedge came the sound of dance music being played somewhere in the estate. He hesitated by the bench and tried to see through the clipped hedge, his head dizzy. Close-packed leaves intervened between him and the distant glow of fairy lights, a crackling barbecue pit, the chatter of voices breaking through the music. Rich White folk having themselves a Friday night do, he told himself.

His knees still trembled and he sat down on the bench. His brown suit was smeared with dust and there were splinters sticking to the material. *We'll catch a fox and put him in a box, a-hunting we will go.* But the music behind the hedge was playing something else, noisy, garish, muted by distance.

What he could not see was that on the vast lawn behind a many-windowed house, two big marquee tents had been erected, flood-lit and strung with coloured lights. From one of the tents came the music and the harsh floodlights scratched at flashing thighs and legs, nylon-clad or bare, and bright mouths panting happily, fingers snapping in rhythm. Most of the menfolk were centred around the other marquee where the liquor was being served. The tennis court was deserted, but heads bobbed like discarded decapitations in the nearby swimming pool. All around lay gardens and clipped trees which had been cared for with clinical attention The fairy lights connected the tents and linked the nearby trees. A fire crackled in the barbecue pit and strings of sausages and skewered

148

mutton chops spluttered and sizzled, while paper plates were being trampled as the meat passed from hand to hand, accompanied by yelps of delight as fingertips scorched.

Beukes sat on the bench outside the hedge and waited for his knees to stop trembling. He rubbed his dizzy forehead and the sounds of revelry behind him grated on his strung nerves like a blunt file. There was no gateway in that stretch of the hedge, so there was no immediate danger of any of the revellers discovering him.

Beyond the hedge, footsteps crunched on a gravel pathway, other steps approached irregularly. A man's voice cried: 'Here she is, chaps. Hey, Vi, why did you run off?'

Beukes was carefully drawing off his coat with his good hand. The left sleeve was black with blood.

'It's that Davey,' a girl's voice complained. 'Can't keep his awful hands to himself.'

'Don't blame him,' a man laughed. 'Come on, forget it and let's go and get another drink. There's gallons of champagne.'

'Who wants champagne? Just because his father's got lots of cash to buy the stuff doesn't mean he can do what he likes. I'm particular who handles me.'

Better not move the shirt, Beukes thought. He only half-heard the voices behind the hedge. It'll protect the wound as the blood dries.

'... Don't act up so, man, Vi. Forget it. Davey was just showing off a bit. After all it *is* his party, hey.'

'Well, that don't give him no right to behave like a bloody kaffir.'

'Oh, Vi ...'

'After all, my daddy's got money too.'

Beukes searched his pockets and found a handkerchief. First aid for wounded, St John's Ambulance, he thought through the ache in his head, his hands trembling.

'Oh, we all know your daddy's in the bloody upper bracket, Vi, but that doesn't mean others aren't. Now come along like a good girl and have a drink with us.'

'Oh, leave me alone. I want to take a walk in the air.'

'Okay then, we'll walk with you.'

Using his good hand and his teeth, Beukes knotted the handkerchief around the bloody shirtsleeve. Somebody was laughing and saying, '. . . champagne . . .' and he thought, I could do with some of that right now, or a stiff brandy. Can't remember when I last tasted brandy. He could not see where the wound was and was afraid of making any sort of examination. Behind him the voices still argued.

'I'd like to be left alone, thank you. Why don't you go and find that Helen Stuttaford?'

Somebody said, 'She's pissed and passed out in the joint.'

'Don't be so vulgar. I'm going to find Frikkie.'

'Oh, God. Him. That farmer, he smells of sheep all the time.'

'Don't be silly, he doesn't go near the farm. I like him, anyway.'

'. . . All go and have some bloody champagne,' another voice cried. 'What's the use of standing here arguing, hey?'

Beukes drew the bloody sleeve into the body of the coat to conceal it and then draped the coat over his shoulder, hiding the wounded arm. He rested on the bench while the voices moved off, the girl still protesting. Now he remembered that only a few days ago he had sat on a bench in a city park and had talked with a nursemaid. Well, he thought suddenly, you're not going to die, man. His mind was now quite clear, although his head still hurt dimly. The murk and shock of panic and flight seemed to have lifted inside him, like mist wiped from a pane. First, you have to get to that doctor and hope he'll fix this arm without too many questions, he told himself. Then you will have to lie low until Monday for Peter, Paul and Michael. Matthew, Mark, Luke, John. Damn, damn, damn, I hope they didn't get Elias. Did they get Elias?

CHAPTER FIFTEEN

The car pulled up outside the Police Station and the Security detectives climbed out. There were trees all around and in the dark they formed big, shapeless shadows against the sky. A gravel driveway with lawns on each side, daubed with a mixture of electric- and moon-light, ran up to the verandah of the station which looked new and was built of orange-red bricks.

The two plain clothes men watched Elias climb out, hand-cuffed, and then they walked him up the driveway. One of them was a tall and burly man, young and good-looking, his hair glossy and carefully arranged, like the wings of a bird. The other was wearing slacks, a windbreaker and a green golf cap, and looked as if he had been called away from some sporting event. He had a reddish-blond moustache and a ruddy face; every few moments he looked at his hands, flexing them.

On the lighted verandah of the Police Station, uniformed police lounged, their holstered pistols clamped to their waists. They looked at Elias as he came up the steps. Inside, the police station was partitioned into two sections, one for Whites and the other for Non-Whites; they went into the bigger Non-White section, and one of the detectives spoke to the desk sergeant. 'You can keep him until morning for us. We will then collect him.'

The desk sergeant looked at Elias and glowered. The two detectives stood by Elias and emptied his pockets dropping what they found there onto the counter: his pipe and tobacco pouch, matches, a cheap pocket watch, a battered passbook.

A bus went past the Police Station along the suburban road; it was almost midnight. Two African constables carrying short spears came in and stood around. They looked at Elias and one of them said something to his companion. The detective in the windbreaker and golf cap yawned and said, 'Hell, I should have been off duty. It is bastards like this who keep one away from home.' He got a half-used packet of cigarettes from the windbreaker and offered one to the young detective.

The sergeant began to make an inventory of the things they had taken from Elias. While he was writing a man came in and staggered to a bench against the wall, he was accompanied by a policeman who shouted abuse at him. The man was groaning and was covered almost from head to foot in blood, which made him look as if somebody had emptied a bucket of red paint over him. He sat there in his bloodstained rags, barefooted and groaning.

'Jesus,' the desk sergeant said, looking over the counter at him. 'What the —— happened to you, *jong*?'

'He's drunk,' the policeman with him, said, 'Friday night, as usual.'

'*Meneer*,' the man said, 'they tackled me.'

The policeman said, '*Meneer*'s mother. There are no misters and sirs here, only bosses.'

'They tackled me,' the wounded man said.

'Who, man?'

'I don't know, boss,' the man groaned. 'They stuck me with a pitchfork.'

'Do you want to make a statement?' the sergeant asked.

A man in a Red Cross uniform came in and knelt by the wounded prisoner and started to examine him, lifting the sticky red rags gingerly. The two Security detectives took no notice of all this. The one in the windbreaker kept on looking at his hands, clenching and unclenching them as if he had a nervous urge to strike something. He bit at the cuticle of one thumb and looked at it closely. The Red Cross nurse draped a sack over the wounded man and led him out. The sergeant finished writing out the property receipt and looked at Elias.

'Can he write?' he asked the young detective.

'Oh, *ja*, he can write,' the one in the sportswear said, 'he's a learned Black.'

The sergeant made Elias sign the receipt and then gave him

152

a copy which he held in his handcuffed hands. The sergeant then called out through a doorway and a policeman came in and jerked his head at the detectives who pushed Elias along ahead of them and behind the policeman. They went out to the back of the Station. It was dark in the yard and the policeman shouted to an African guard who clanked out of the dark like a ghost in a topi, dangling a bunch of keys.

He looked at Elias in the starlit dark and said, 'You must get a blanket.'

'What did he say? asked one of the detectives.

'A blanket,' the policeman said.

'No blankets. We will be fetching him soon. Lock him up, *jong.*'

They all crossed the yard to a part lighted by a single bulb above a cell door. The turnkey unlocked the door and the detectives pushed Elias inside. There was a light burning in a bulb behind a rectangle of thick plate glass in the cell, and it cast a dim glow, like light seen through water.

As soon as he was alone, Elias inspected the cell for any possibility of escape. He hardly expected to find any in that small, sealed box, but he looked nevertheless. It did not take him long to discover that he was trapped, fast as a fly in a bottle.

Elias sat down on the floor in his handcuffs thinking, now it has come to this. He wondered first how the police had come to discover the meeting place. They were very up-to-date in their methods; one could not tell where they would move next. He hoped Beukes had got away from them. He had heard somebody shoot, let it not be that he was shot. They were very quick to shoot. If they had caught him surely they would have brought them along together. Perhaps . . . perhaps he had got away. He would be alone now, without any contacts except those few of his own people, and one already missing. What a damage all this was – until somebody came along to sort matters out and establish the section again.

They would want him to talk. They are going to hurt you,

Elias Tekwane, he told himself. Do not think about it now, it is no use thinking about it now. Think about something else.

He looked around the cell again: he had been in a cell such as this before, the time of the strike after he'd been clubbed and knocked unconscious. After that he had been charged with breaking his contract and endorsed out of the city to a transit labour camp.

He recalled that camp now, seeing in his mind's eye the bleak rows of shabby prefabricated huts, the makeshift tents flapping like broken wings. It had been crowded with displaced persons, the discarded unemployed; people who no longer had permission to work in the 'White' areas; labourers who had broken their contract for some reason or another; ex-convicts who had been refused leave to earn a living in the towns. Whole families had occupied the bleak, grey one-roomed houses: the wives and children of 'surplus labour' had moved there to join their menfolk, rather than remain separated.

When they had arrived no-one had known what to do, Elias recalled. They had all stood by the old bus which had brought them and waited in the cold wind that blew in from the hills, until some men had come along and looked at their papers. Most of the time they had sat around wondering what would become of them. All around were the bare eroded hills, like the decayed teeth of a giant, with women in tattered blankets scratching the stony earth, hoping to grow something there. They had been like mechanical scarecrows on the hillsides, but the birds had ignored them.

There had been nothing to eat; those who could afford some food had had to feed their families. After waiting some time, however, Elias had teamed up with a man called Mdlaka. He had managed to get work on a gang doing road repairs for the provincial authorities, because he was young and strong.

'We see you,' this Mdlaka had said. 'Why are you here?'

'I was in a strike,' Elias had told him. 'The *amabulu*, the Whites, would not let me stay in the city after that.'

'A strike?' Mdlaka had asked. 'When was that?'

Elias had told him and Mdlaka had nodded, with a wise expression in his eyes. Elias had been young then and had found this man somewhat curious. 'I was at this laundry, working at the steam machines,' he had explained.

It was very hard work on the roads, but he had been paid a few shillings for a week's work, so that he could buy a sack of meal and some tobacco and perhaps a few odds and ends. Not everybody had been able to get work and most of the people in the camp had had to hang about and hope for the best. There had been old people too, pensioners who were no longer of value in the big city: everybody had been dumped there like broken and useless machinery.

'That you were in a strike is interesting,' Mdlaka had said. 'I myself was given six months in prison for political offences. The *amabulu* do not tolerate our people who talk to others of opposing their government. So I was given the six months for leading people in what they called a riotous assembly. From the prison I was sent right here, without being able to see my people.'

'What was the assembly for then?' Elias had asked, feeling rather silly and inexperienced. It had been the rest period and he was sitting by the roadside with Mdlaka.

'Listen,' Mdlaka had said, 'I'll explain it to you ...'

There were nine men on the work gang. One of them was old Tsatsu who was practically their grandfather. It was not pleasant to see such an old man having to work on the roads with men who were young enough to be his grandchildren. But if a man did not accept work when the chance came, he had to starve with the rest of what officialdom referred to as the 'efflux'.

One day when the foreman from the provincial council had blown his whistle for everyone to fall in after the rest break, old Tsatsu had not got up from the heap of rubble where he was resting.

'What's the matter with that old *bliksem*?' the foreman had asked. 'This is no time to sleep.'

A man who had gone over to wake him had come back saying, 'He is not asleep. He has gone to his ancestors, and may they receive him with more kindness than he has met with in this world.' The old man had lain on the heap of rubble like a bundle of discarded old clothes.

Everybody in the camp had gone to his funeral although few had known where old Tsatsu was from or who his family was. He had just been an old man who had worked himself to death in order to stay alive. He had been wrapped in a blanket, the cleanest and least torn they could find, and buried on a hillside away from the camp. Other people had been buried there, including some children. Those who had been in the camp before Elias had started the graveyard, and those who died afterwards had just followed on. It was like a place where the crumbs of humanity were brushed away under a carpet of stony earth.

That had also been the time when Elias had listened to Mdlaka in all seriousness. It was Mdlaka who had conducted the funeral since there had been no religious man in the camp and, after all, Mdlaka spoke well. Everybody had listened to him that day on the hillside with the weathered and cracked headboards sprouting from the earth like strange dry plants, and the wind reaching from the hills like the cold hands of death.

Afterwards there had been a meeting to decide who would take Tsatsu's place on the road gang.

Sometime later when the authorities were recruiting again for some workers for this city, Elias had managed to get signed on. After his arrival he had gone, with a letter written by Mdlaka on a scrap of wrapping-paper, to the organization that Mdlaka had spoken of.

That was a long time ago, Elias thought. And now it had come to this. But remembering Mdlaka and Tsatsu the old man again he had no regrets, and knew that he would have done everything over again, given the opportunity.

CHAPTER SIXTEEN

Outside, a dust-wagon passed, the horse's hooves clopping on the street, while the fading afternoon measured itself away in a diminishing bar of yellow light, edging across the linoleum floor, past a small coffee-table and a framed print of brown mountain ranges. The waiting-room was the front of a private house, bare except for a row of chairs, the table with the inevitable copies of ancient magazines, thumbed and curly bound editions of the *Overseas Daily Mirror* and *Femina*. There was no news; you had to be contented with history.

Beukes sat in one of the chairs, his bloody sleeve hidden under his jacket which was buttoned at the waist. His head ached, he felt feverish and his arm throbbed, as he waited with pain and impatience for his turn to see the doctor.

There were two other patients before him: an old man in a thick overcoat in spite of the warm afternoon, his mouth trembling with ague, eyes hollow and watery, and a child in a clean, brushed suit wearing a man's necktie, accompanied by his mother. The child sucked his thumb and dribbled onto his tie as he stared at Beukes. The room smelled faintly of disinfectant.

Beukes had decided to visit the doctor as any other patient would: one aroused less suspicion that way. The walking wounded, he imagined with a sense of drama, went to aid stations under the trees where the jeeps were parked and the waiting stretcher-bearers chewed gum. Later the cast of actors would appear on the screen, and the lights would go on. Real life would return in the form of peanut shells on the floor; the ice-cream cartons.

The child, sucking its thumb and dribbling onto the front of the Sunday suit, was staring at Beukes with enquiring eyes.

The mother's look was surreptitiously accusing, she watched him out of the corners of her eyes whenever she made the child remove his thumb. She took in the drawn, stubbled face, the dull copper-brown eyes, and mistook weariness for bravado in the pinched upper lip. The wounded arm was hidden under the coat, but there was a dark stain of dried blood on the shirtsleeve that slipped into sight: a ruffian who had been involved in some drunken brawl with knives, she decided.

You don't turn up at the doctor's in the middle of the night announcing that you are on the run from the police, Beukes thought. Besides, he did not know the doctor's home address. He had recalled that sometime, long ago, this doctor had given a donation to the funds of the organization; he had called here at the surgery with another member. But that had been a long time ago, when one could go around collecting from sympathizers with a measure of certainty. Had the doctor changed, now that everything had become illegal? He would have to take a chance, think up some legitimate reason for his wound. In the world of the oppressed a wound over the week-end was as common as a leaking roof. It throbbed and ached and he forced down impatience, waiting for his turn.

The old man had fallen asleep in his chair, but his mouth still trembled. The woman admonished the thumb-sucking child once again, whispering threats of nasty medicine if he persisted. She peered at Beukes, silently challenging him to prove her wrong.

At last the surgery door opened and a man came out, clutching a bottle of brown liquid. Behind him, a dark-skinned woman with a carefully-made-up face and a white smock, called: 'Next'.

The mother leapt to her feet as if she thought Beukes or the old man would jump the queue, and hurried through the door, past the nurse, dragging the child behind her. The old man shook in his chair and dozed on. The bar of yellow light dwindled on the wall. Another patient came in and hesitated then went self-consciously to a chair.

After what seemed a very long time, the doctor was saying, 'Oh, it's Mister-er-Benjamin, isn't it?' He peered through horn-rimmed glasses and played with a sphygmomonameter. Behind and around him were ranged the tools of his trade: the couch and stirrups like a modern equivalent of a medieval rack, glass cases full of dangerous-looking needles and syringes, glass-stoppered jars and bottles which might have held poison. But in his starched white coat, small, plump and yellow, his hair like grey silk, he was antiseptic, without menace. The cheerful eyes behind the round lenses set the patient at ease; long years of practice had given him a reassuring air.

'Beukes. The name's Beukes.' He did not mind the mistake: nowadays one changed names the way one changed a shirt.

'Of course,' the doctor said. 'Beukes. You came to visit me once before. It wasn't the illness, was it? No, I remember now.' He motioned to a chair and said to the dark woman, 'Don't bother about a card for this patient, nurse.'

Beukes was in the chair and the nurse unbuttoned his coat. The doctor hovered, smelling of a mixture of tobacco and ether. 'Hmmm, hmmm, you seem to have hurt yourself.'

The nurse cut away the shirtsleeve and it dropped like the dry moulting skin of a brown snake among the used swabs in a bin. Beukes winced as the wound was exposed; he did not look at it.

The doctor smiled at him through the horn-rimmed glasses: 'Hmm, a nasty gash. Nurse, I think we shall need a few stitches there. If you would clean it out.'

'A-er-accident,' Beukes offered to explain, but he was gagged by a thermometer and the nurse probed gingerly but efficiently at his arm. When the thermometer was removed, Beukes said, 'Doctor, if you could spare a moment in private?'

'Of course, Mister Beukes. But first we'll get you fixed up, eh?' He brandished a little skein of suture and smiled with his round, yellow face. 'So, what have you been doing since I last saw you?' But he did not give Beukes a chance to think of an alibi. 'Don't bother to talk if you don't feel like it. You must have a headache.' He said something to the nurse about a local anaesthetic. 'Just a bad gash, some of your flesh torn away.'

'It happened last night,' Beukes said. 'I couldn't find a doctor.'

'That's all right. I don't suppose you could go to the casualty ward at a hospital either, certainly not without having to go through a lot of formalities.' He smiled all the time, his eyes bright as a bird's behind the spectacles. The nurse worked expertly and smelled of perfume and cosmetics, unlike the doctor.

At last the doctor said, 'There,' and rinsed his hands in a corner sink. The nurse was busy clearing things away. He came back to Beukes and beamed, drying his hands. 'Does your arm feel numb?' he asked. 'That's just because we had to deaden it a little. I'll give you some tablets in case there's some fever. You will have to rest a few days, of course.' He turned to the nurse. 'Nurse, if you would put on the kettle, we might have some tea, eh?'

When the nurse had gone through a door to another part of the house, the doctor sat down behind his desk, smiling at Beukes across a box of record cards, prescription pads and the blood-pressure apparatus.

Beukes said, his arm feeling like something apart from the rest of him, 'Doctor, do you have to report accidents?' He needed to absolve the doctor from any complicity.

'Under normal circumstances, yes, I suppose so.' He produced a cigarette case, flicked it open and offered it to Beukes, then he produced a lighter. They sat there with the smoke between them.

'Well, it's like this . . .' Beukes started to say.

But the doctor broke up the smoke with a small, plump hand and said through the gap: 'Mister Beukes, I can tell a gunshot wound, even a flesh wound, when I see one, although I do not have the opportunity of treating many. The trenchlike wound, not made by a knife, along your forearm. The police?'

Beukes nodded. The doctor said, 'Yes, one could guess so.

Things have been happening in the country recently, haven't they? Well, the law says I should report suspicious wounds and so on.'

'Will you obey the law?'

The doctor looked at his cigarette and then back at Beukes. 'If the community is given the opportunity of participating in making the law, then they have a moral obligation to obey it,' he said. 'But if the law is made for them, without their consent or participation, then it's a different matter.' He paused and sat back in his chair. 'However, even under the circumstances prevailing in our country, I must ask myself, what does this law or that law defend, even if I did not help to make it. If the law punishes a crime, murder, rape, then I could bring myself to assist it. I would consider reporting a murder, a case of assault. But if the law defends injustice, prosecutes and persecutes those who fight injustice, then I am under no obligation to uphold it. They have actually given us an opportunity to pick and choose. Things happen in our country, Mister Beukes. Injustice prevails, and there are people who have the nerve enough to defy it. Pehaps I have been waiting for the opportunity to put my penny in the hat as well.' He smiled at Beukes with a look of triumph. It was as if he had been waiting a long time to make a speech and now the opportune moment had come. 'Now that I have delivered myself of that homily, we can have some tea. The nurse will be along with it shortly.' He smiled. 'I am sorry if you have had to be a sort of – er – captive audience to my childish pronouncements.'

'You are taking a chance, doctor,' Beukes said. 'We appreciate it.'

'Chance?' the doctor smiled. 'Yes, I suppose so. But it takes me back to my student days. We were quite adventurous then.' He stood up suddenly and went around the desk to a cupboard. 'There might be something else I can do for you.'

Outside, the evening stained the sky with its purple dye and slowly smothered the glow of the late sunset that had formed a backdrop for the rampart of suburban housing. The neon haze of the city glowed far off, like the aftermath of an aerial attack. Outside a cinema for Non-Whites a queue moved slowly past the ticket-box. A drunk sat on the kerbside. Saturday night was cinema night and the night for merriment. A newspaper placard said: 'Security Chief on Underground Leaflets,' and Beukes bought a paper from a little boy in a dirty singlet, and moved on past the queue. A sign of an easel in the foyer stated: 'For children under sixteen and Non-Whites.' In his floppy tweed jacket he was just another young man going somewhere, or making up his mind to buy a ticket.

The tweed jacket he had acquired from the doctor, who had produced it from the cupboard. 'My wife collects for a sale in aid of spastics,' he said, holding the coat as if he were a bullfighter. 'You don't mind, do you? It might be a little on the large side. Somebody left it here for the sale, but I don't suppose it will be missed.'

'It is very good of you,' Beukes had said, standing in the surgery in his shirt with only one sleeve. 'It will come in handy, you bet.'

The doctor had helped him transfer the contents of his own stained coat to the other. They had sat at the desk while the nurse poured tea. She was unperturbed, as if mysterious young men with mysterious wounds which were not recorded, were part of the routine: undernourishment, scrofula, the common cold. Then, remembering the old man who dozed shakily in the waiting-room, Beukes had emptied his cup hurriedly and had stood up, saying, 'Doctor, I must go. You have things to do, hey.'

'Take the pills every four hours if you get a headache,' the doctor had said, rising too. 'I've put them in the coat pocket. It was nice to see you again after all this time, Mister Beukes. You should rest the arm, and in actual fact you ought to come back in about three weeks so that I can look at the stitches.' He had looked at Beukes with a mixture of enquiry and hope; perhaps he would have another of his homilies to deliver.

Beukes had nodded, smiling, while the nurse had helped him into the tweed. It was a little baggy under the arms and around the chest, but it would pass: nobody noticed second-hand clothing on a member of a second-class people. He had said, 'I will try to come. I reckon you know how it is, doctor.'

'Yes, I think I understand,' the doctor had smiled, the light glinting on his spectacles. 'Take good care of yourself.'

The evening traffic rolled past, to and from the centre of the city. Beukes decided not to return to Tommy's: one had to keep on changing addresses. Was Tommy still around? He recalled saying to Tommy, just as the latter was getting ready to leave for work, 'If I'm not here when you get back, don't worry, chum.' Tommy had stood there in his black dress-trousers and checked coat, looking glum.

'All the best then, Bukey boy,' he had said. Then added, 'I'll see you in my dreams.' He would never give up talking with the vocabulary of popular songs.

Beukes looked at the newspaper. The woman who had murdered her husband had returned to the front page, next to the report which stated that the Security Police had raided and searched places all over the country. The hunt was up, of course. No names were mentioned, but those would come later as the news filtered through and more statements were made. Not Frances, he thought, not Frances. Don't let them have found out about me. The serious national news was padded with the announcements of officialdom. 'The Minister of Defence stated in the House ... It was announced last night by the Commissioner of Police ... The Minister of the Interior, of Coloured Affairs, Asiatic Affairs ...' Ministerial statements disguised facts, they could dismiss anything as speculation, misreporting, or threaten a breach of the Secrets Act.

He decided to go direct to April's. That would be a fifteen-cent bus ride from where he was. He waited at a bus-stop, counting change in his pocket, the newspaper tucked under the wounded arm, held against his side ... a sling might arouse attention. The arm felt better now, stitched and padded and warm. He waited for the bus and again felt as exposed as a fly on a wall. Whites-Only buses passed and he cursed in his mind, waiting for the other. It was full of the Saturday evening crowd, race-goers analysing the fields they had left behind, but he found a seat and sat guarding his arm.

Passengers dropped off, the suburb dwindled and they rolled along a stretch of road through the ranks of segregated housing with walls peeling like diseased skin, while the evening filtered along the roofs, along the sandy paths, the dark-skinned children staring out over fences like shabby glove-puppets. A factory passed greyly by, deserted; a municipal market with the stalls empty and shut; a sign at the approach to a cement and brick works: *Drive Carefully, Natives Crossing Ahead*. But there was nobody, and the bus shook onwards. Another suburb grew out of the gathering dusk: the stereotyped cottages with streets grandiloquently named after various flowers; a grocery store clamped for safety behind bars and metal grilles, like a manifestation of the moral decay of its customers.

April's was a small brick cottage to which had been attached a rough workshop. A metal sign painted by an unskilled hand said, *Panel Beating, Motor Repairs*. In the yard an old mongrel, tethered to a rusty axle, kept guard over the disconnected parts of motor cars, piles of worn tyres, the wire washlines. It growled at Beukes, through broken teeth. He went around the dog and over to the workshop.

In the open workshop a van was jacked up, a man's greasily overalled legs jutted over from under it in the light of a lamp at the end of a cable. The trunkless legs reminded Beukes of the house where he had last seen Elias, and he wondered bleakly about the fate of his friend. From under the van came sounds associated with car repairs. From beyond the house and the workshop came the sound of hymn-singing inside a meeting-hall of Seventh Day Adventists. The shadows inched into the workshop, across the oil-stained floor strewn with the iron bowels of transport, oil cans, spanners. Against the wall leaned a dented mudguard, but it did not belong to the van.

Beukes stood in the big doorway and called, 'Henny, Henny April, you old chancer.'

The legs moved outward and the torso contorted so that a head and face, smudged with grease, could emerge. 'Old Buke,' the smudged face said. 'Jesus Christ Almighty, is it you then, hey?'

He clambered to his feet, a small man with bad teeth and a big smile that split his face like a blotched melon. He rubbed his hands on the overalls and then on some waste, looked at them, changed his mind about shaking hands, and said: 'Jesus bloody Christ, glad to see you, chummy.' Blasphemy was as natural to his vocabulary as hair to a dog. 'I was reading the papers and I thought to myself, Christ, I hope old bloody goddamn Buke isn't in no trouble. Remember that last game of draughts we played? Are you okay, pal? Goddamnit.'

'I'm okay,' Beukes told him. He looked at the van. 'Did you get my message? Is the bus in working order?'

'She's going to be, by Monday anyway, even if I have to work all of tonight and tomorrow.'

'What's wrong with her?'

'Never mind that van,' Henny April said. 'It will be okay, man. Let's go into the house, hey.'

They went out of the workshop together. Across the roofs and fences the hymns were carried on the lamplight. Henny April led the way towards the door of the cottage. 'You think it will be okay going at this time?' Beukes asked him.

Henny April asked: 'You mean that the law will be laying out *mos* for us?'

'Something like that. They might not know our faces, but they might be stopping cars on the road out.'

Henny April laughed and said: 'Don't you give a goddamn, Buke. The johns are not going to get this boy. Jesus, no. I been in this business a long time, hey. If you worry about the law too much, you never get things done.'

'Business' was not only repairing cars, Beukes knew. It also involved the transportation of various unregistered or illegally acquired cargoes, inanimate as well as human, like the contents of plundered warehouses which had to be disposed of; Asiatics who did not have the necessary official permits to cross provincial borders. Such affairs could be negotiated with this little man with the face like a melon, the bad teeth and the sacreligious punctuations in his conversation.

He looked about. 'They forcing more and more people out of the city and making them move here. And not enough houses. It's getting like a dumping-ground for human beings.'

He put a finger to a nostril and blew his nose into the dust of the yard. It was like a demonstration of contempt for authority. He took Beukes heartily by the arm, but withdrew it quickly as the young man winced.

'What's up, Buke?' he asked, looking into the stubbled face, the peaked eyes. 'Your arm sore?'

'I got hurt a little,' Beukes told him. 'It's nothing.'

'You do look *mos* kind of sickish. Well, come inside and we'll have something.' He did not pursue the matter of the wounded arm: in the 'business' the fewer questions asked the more confidence gained.

They were in a small living-room crammed with odds and ends of furniture as well as children. There was an oval table laden with crockery surrounded by chairs and benches with children squeezed onto them, eating; a sideboard with a cracked mirror; cardboard boxes fastened with belts and old neckties piled in a corner; under a sagging settee one could see suitcases; in other corners were the spare parts of automobiles. From the kitchen came the smell of cooking.

'Here's uncle,' Henny April announced to the children. He gestured towards the settee and said, 'Siddown, pal,' and while Beukes squeezed past the circle of children, patting sundry kinky heads, he shouted towards the kitchen: 'Maria, we got a visitor, come and see.'

'I am coming,' a woman's deep voice called back.

The children ate on in disciplined silence, as if they had

been trained that silence was necessary for the survival of the 'business' and the assurance of further suppers. Only shy smiles and whispered observations indicated that they had met this uncle before. Beukes sat on the settee and wondered whether the old boxes and suitcases had been opened since the last time he had been there. But the mystery of what they contained would probably never be solved in his presence.

From the kitchen came a big African woman. She was made even bigger by advanced pregnancy which she carried under a stained apron. She wore an old beret and held a long spoon like a spear at the trail.

She cried, 'My, my, it is that Beukes,' while he stood up and smiled at her.

'How are you, Maria?'

She laughed boomingly, and gestured with the spoon at the swollen belly. 'Auw! You see how it is, Beukes. That Henny.' She laughed again and said, 'You must eat, yes.' Then to her husband: 'Make place for him, you.'

Beukes said, 'I didn't mean to turn up tonight. I should have come on Monday, but you know how it is with us.'

'I know, man,' the woman smiled; she might have been referring to her condition. 'But do not worry. We will fix you up.'

Henny April was dismissing those children who had finished supper so that Beukes could sit at the table. He said, 'You can have our bed. Maria and me can move in with the children.'

'You must be mad,' Beukes told him. 'I will fit in with these lighties.'

'He has a bad arm,' Henny April told his wife.

'It's nothing,' Beukes said. 'The children won't get in my way.'

'Are you certain of it?' Maria asked. 'It's easy for us to move.'

'I'll be awright,' Beukes said. 'Don't make a fuss. It's only tonight and tomorrow night.'

'Sit then and eat,' the woman said. 'Are you feeling good? You look a little sick.'

'The doctor gave me some tablets for my headache. If I can have some water first. Otherwise everything is ship-shape.'

Beukes sat at the table and Henny April sat opposite him while Maria brought in plates of food. The children had moved off little by little into another part of the house, their murmurs drifting into the room. Beukes had always been awed by this little man's ability to procreate so many children.

'Everything will be okay, by God,' Henny April said as they ate. 'Not to worry, *ou* Buke.' He brandished a fork. 'There was a time, hey, when the law they had road-blocks up and I brought some stuff through right under their noses. Loco-weed, man.'

'Well,' Beukes said, 'from Monday morning these fellows will be in your hands. It's as far as the first point – you know where it is. After that, somebody else will take over.'

'Not to worry, Buke, not to worry,' the little man said, smiling with his bad teeth. 'Leave it to Brother Henny, hey. Jesus, me, I don't boast, but I get things done.' He gestured again with his fork, taking in the crowded room, the unidentifiable boxes and suitcases, his big wife's numerous pregnancies, past and future. 'Just relax, pal. Later on we can play some draughts. You know I like my game of draughts.'

CHAPTER SEVENTEEN

Pain was like a devil which had usurped his body. It was wrenching in his wrists and hands and the sockets of his shoulders as he dangled with all the weight on the handcuffs that shackled him to the staple in the wall. It was his body, battered and bruised by the pistol barrel, and in his legs, his skinned shins, which would not hold his weight. There was a taste of pain in his mouth where the blood had replaced saliva. His whole body was held together on a framework of pain and he was thirsty. His head dangled on his chest: he could see his torn shirt, his waistband – they had taken away his belt – all blurred through puffed eyes, so he knew vaguely that he was alive. He tried to stand up straight, but his legs were pierced by nails, and he sagged again on the manacles. He was only dimly aware of the room, the grey walls, the stone floor, a cigarette butt flung aside and crushed like an insect, dead; but the room seemed to move, the walls bulged and undulated, the floor stirred as if on rollers. He was thirsty.

He licked his dry, swollen lips with a harsh tongue and said aloud, painfully: 'Think, think of something else, think of anything.'

He was a child and they all ran along the railway tracks through the dust, waving their hands as the windows blinked past, faces stared down at him for an instant and then were gone. Then it was autumn. The grass was still green, and at that time the evenings were best. There was already a chill in the air, a touch of cool rain, especially in the valleys. They were sitting around the fires in front of the homesteads. He could see the smoke, as if drawn by a fairy hand, slowly drifting down the valley. The bird songs died out first and then the voices of the children. He would sleep peacefully because now there was hardly any work to do in the fields . . .

The door crashed open and the two detectives came down the steps. Elias looked up heavily and saw them as through a defective windowpane: their faces swelled and contracted, elongated and blurred. They did not say anything and the one with the glossy hair unlocked the manacles which held him to the staples. They did not bother to hold him up and he felt his legs give with pain as the weight of his body came down on the floor. He fell on his face and tried to raise himself on his hands which were held in the second pair of handcuffs. After a struggle he was able to sit up.

Then the sportsman said, 'Well, get up, *jong*.'

'My legs, they hurt,' Elias told him, speaking with the dry, thick mouth. He could still smell the urine in his clothes.

'We'll give you hurt,' the sportsman said.

They each took him under the arms and he was paddled up to the door, out of the room, stumbling, trying to use his legs, gasping with the pain in them, stumbling and flopping like a doll all the way to another room. It was little bigger than a broom cupboard and there was a table and two chairs in it. They thrust him into one of the chairs and the glossy-haired one sat down in the other. The sportsman lit a cigarette while the other opened a pad which was on the table.

'Well, do you want to tell everything now?' the young one asked, tapping the pad with a ball-point pen, staring at Elias with angry eyes.

Elias said huskily, 'Can I have some water? I am thirsty.'

The sportsman said, 'Shit. Do you think this is a hotel? Talk, and then you might get some water.'

The young man held his pen ready, as if he was impatient to set down what Elias was about to say. 'So you are going to tell us all then?'

Elias looked at them, seeing them hazily, far away, and saw that they were like rags from which all the water of humanity had been squeezed. He said with his thick tongue. 'You see, it is impossible. I cannot tell you anything.'

The young one stared at Elias with eyes that were now flat and expressionless as a reptile's. He put his pen away in the breast pocket of his jacket, still staring at Elias, then buttoned his jacket and stood up. He looked at the sportsman then, talking with his flat eyes.

The sportsman dragged Elias out of the chair and he fell on the floor again. Once more they seized him by his armpits and hauled him out of the tiny room. They took him down the corridor into another room which was bigger and had several chairs, tables, some unusual equipment. They dropped him into a chair and the young one unlocked one wrist and then dragged Elias's arms behind the chair and shackled his hands there.

The sportsman said, 'You better talk, kaffir.'

Even with the pain, Elias felt the insult more than the fear, so he said, 'It is no use, it is no use.'

The glossy-haired one said, his voice shrill with menace, 'Hear us, we do not care, if you don't tell us, we will kill you.'

The sportsman hit Elias in the face then beat him up methodically, working on him at close quarters and a vast blue-blackness seemed to be coming towards him through the pain, an almost welcoming darkness. His mouth tasted of fresh blood again and his head seemed to be tearing free of his neck. He felt himself sliding away into the darkness that roared like a waterfall.

The sportsman said, as if in an echo-chamber, 'It's okay, you won't go to sleep, you baboon.'

But Elias fell over, taking the chair with him, falling heavily, so that the chair broke. The sportsman cursed and grabbed part of the chair and hit Elias across the head with it.

'Hurry up and talk, baboon,' the one with the glossy hair said, smoking a cigarette. 'You can stay here until you tell us everything or get killed, do you hear?'

Elias lay on the floor and sailed away somewhere. He had the feeling that there was nothing to do but hope that pain would disappear, and he waited for it to slide back out of reach. His silence, his resolve, now seemed to take on the form of a force within him: the amalgam of pain and brutality atomized slowly into the gathering ghosts of his many ancestors which seemed to insulate him from pain. Pain was there, yes, but somehow something apart, a satellite revolving the planet of his being, his mind, which was full of the faraway ululations, the rattle of spears on shields, the tramp of thousands of feet.

They dragged him, bloody, to another chair. Somebody hurled water into his dough-puffy face, but it could have been acid, for his skin burned at the touch of it. Blood and water dribbled down his neck.

'We can do better,' somebody was saying.

Think of something, the pain said; something in which you believe, like love. Old Tsatsu was dead on a heap of rubble by the road, a collapsed dummy, something unimportant left aside. 'He is not asleep, but has gone to his ancestors and may they receive him with more kindness than he has met in this world.' The people sang on the dreary hillside and the wind carried away their voices like dry leaves. The sick miner walked, thin and bent, staring out of dead eyes while he coughed and spat with the disease that ate him up, as a rat would eat cheese. 'He has been bewitched,' the children cried. Bewitched? Far down in the darkness, darker then any tomb, another miner was dispersed beyond recognition under infinite tons of fallen rock and gold: yellow gold, soft as putty, which could turn the hearts of men into pitiless organs of brass.

He was being manhandled. Now there was another darkness as a sack was dragged over his head. They pulled off his trousers and underpants. He was suspended grotesquely, with his arms about his drawn-up legs and a broom handle above his elbows and below his knees. The sportsman had fixed certain electrical apparatus into a wall plug. Far away the tramp of thousands of feet drummed on the crackling earth, the rattle of spears and shields came across the long, hazy distance with the cries.

He screamed inside the sack.

The glossy-haired one cranked the handle of the magneto while the sportsman ran the electrodes against bare legs, genitals.

Elias screamed. He had anticipated violence, but not this, not this. Talk, talk, talk, his mind told him while his body jerked and jigged like a broken puppet on badly-manipulated strings. But far, far away the ghosts gathered, the feathers bobbed and swayed, the leopard tails swung, and the sun, like a yellow lantern in the resistant sky, glanced like lightning from the hammered spearblades.

His flesh burned and scorched and his limbs jerked and twitched and fell away from him, jolting and leaping in some fantastic dance which only horror linked to him. A thousand worms writhed under his skin and broke through the surface of his flesh, each one of them shrieking in the black darkness, while far away the ghosts drifted along the hazy horizon and beckoned to him to come to join them.

After a time the detectives stood back and jerked the sack from his head. They saw a shabby mask, a face puffed into swollen blankness, like the face of a drowned man.

They seized him and dragged him from the room, trouser-less, his shirt bloody and ripped from the previous beating, back to the basement from which they had fetched him, and dropped him on the stone steps, slamming the heavy door and locking it on him.

The edge of a stone step ground into his temple, but the feeling of it was something apart. Nothing was real, not even pain, not even the bitter cud of humiliation in his mouth. Inside his hollow mind a single word flapped around like a torn rag in a wind-swept sand-lot: talk, talk, talk.

The stone step was actually warm against his face. Footsteps ran past him and the smell of dust on paving was in his nostrils; blood trickled into his neck from his scalp, where the policeman's club had caught him on the morning of the strike meeting. He was leaving home and his mother, small and homely – there was ochre powder on her face – gave him the parcel of roasted potatoes and the wiry chicken they had dared to butcher the night before: these were meant for him to eat on the road to the city. The old bus waited, puttering and wheezing like a tired old man, to drive the contracted workers to the main railway station. His mother did not cry, as perhaps other mothers would have done. Instead, she touched him with a hand and said, 'Hauw! you are a man now, my son.' The womenfolk stood by the roadside, watching the bus cough away into the distance; the men watched them recede into the brown dust mingled with the blue-grey exhaust smoke. That was when he had remembered that he had not packed the book from which he had first learned to read in English. But he had done many things since then, and read many books. The brown hills, the village, Wasserman's store, sprang into view for an instant on the flickering screen of his mind and then were gone.

Now only the black crows gathered over the battlefield. *Uya kuhlasela-pi na? Where wilt thou now wage war?* The ghosts of his ancestors beckoned from afar.

The Major said, 'You know your trouble? You are stupid. You can save yourself much distress, man. Have you not had enough?'

'He's making a bladdy fool of us,' the sportsman said. He looked at Elias. 'We are at war, and your life really means nothing to us.'

The glossy-haired one said 'If you die we can always say you committed suicide. After talking.'

The Major said again, 'You are stupid, so we have to knock some bloody sense into you.'

He got up and went to the door of the room. The air was blue with cigarette smoke and the two detectives were coatless. The Major was wearing an executive suit and the starched cuffs of his shirt peeped from his coat sleeves; he looked large and oval and official. He hesitated for a moment at the door, nodded to the two detectives, and then went out.

The glossy-haired one said, 'Give it to him good this time, the ——ing baboon.'

There was the darkness of the sack again. Talk, talk, talk. But the ghosts waited for him on some far horizon. No words came, only the screaming of many crows circling the battlefield. *Wahlula amakosi! Thou hast conquered the Kings!* The far figures moved along the far horizon. *He! Uya kuhlasela-pi na? Yes, where wilt thou now wage war?* Far, far, his ancestors gathered on the misty horizon, their spears sparkling like diamonds in the exploding sun. Somebody came out of the bright haze and touched him with a hand. His mind called out 'Mother'. From afar came the rushing sound of trampling feet.

CHAPTER EIGHTEEN

There was not much time to wait. Henny April had packed some mysterious suitcases into the van and Maria had provided a shopping-bag of food for the journey. Peter and Michael sat on the settee in the front room. They were young Africans, one of them wearing a straw boater, and each had a bundle held on his lap. It was early in the morning, towards dawn, and the electric light made their faces look yellow and intent. Maria sat at the table and spoke to them heartily in the vernacular and they replied, laughing and shaking their heads, shyly avoiding her eyes. They had turned up some hours before, and the old dog in the yard had wakened the house with its barking.

Beukes had slept fitfully in the children's room amid a maze of wooden and metal bunks, clothes dangling like bats in the dark, scattered shoes. He had stayed indoors all Sunday while Henny April had worked on the van. The pain in his arm had subsided to a gentle, untroublesome ache. In the afternoon the children, scrubbed and shiny, had been sent off to the local Sunday-school. Later in the evening, Henny April had announced that the van was ready to go like a bomb. Then they had sat at the table in the front, playing draughts far into the night. He had tried to read before feeling asleep, but it had been one of the children's books: *The Young Book of Pirates*. Henny must be preparing his offspring for their future careers, he had thought, amused; the children would probably inherit the 'business' from their father. Afterwards he had drifted off to sleep.

He had wakened early in the morning when the dog started barking. The children had woken up too, and he had seen their eyes, bright as those of mice, in the darkness before he had reached out to turn on the light, all of them quiet, listening calmly. Had they been taught that there was no benefit in panic at the sound of alarm? He had heard Henny going to the front door just as the knocking came. The light had gone on in the front room, voices had mumbled and then Henny had come into the room in his long, grimy underwear to tell him that the two men had arrived.

Now they were sitting on the settee talking to Maria while Beukes wondered about the third one. He had shaken hands with them, and one of them, the one called Michael, had asked: 'How is Elias?'

Beukes had said, 'I believe he is all right.' He wondered how the young man knew about him and Elias. It's all too shaky, he thought, but dismissed suspicion like an intruder from his mind. One has to go through with it, he told himself. 'There is another man due,' he told them. 'We will wait for him.'

'We should go with the daylight, hey,' Henny April said, while they ate bowls of porridge at the table. He was wearing washed-out overalls and a cloth cap. The children remained in bed. 'Will he come?'

'Why not?' Beukes asked. 'These two comrades turned up.' He had already told them who would meet them when they arrived at their destination and that they should use their code names all the time. 'The other man is Paul,' he had said.

The night turned grey and dawn approached warmly; over-head the darkness drifted slowly away like the smoke of a recent battle. Soon, Beukes thought, the mornings will be colder and then we'll have autumn. Hell, I wonder how we will operate in the winter? Will we operate at all, anyway? If they've taken Elias, who will get in touch with me? But Elias would not be the only one who knew of him; somewhere there must be another. He would leave a message with Polsky, the pharmacist.

Henny April went out to potter around the van to pass the time. Maria brought a pot of coffee and they drank it from mugs. The window was grey, but the dawn did not add yet to the lamplight that splashed over the clutter in the front room: the piled boxes, the spare parts, the sideboard with the cracked mirror. They might have taken him, this Paul, Beukes thought. If they have, they might have made him talk, and then they'd know about him, Peter and Michael, Henny April, and big Maria, the children. Don't let that happen, he whispered inside himself, don't let that happen. *A-hunting we will go.* The Security people would be very active now, the lights on in the little brown offices, over the barred gateways, the Public Works crockery. He sat there, in his baggy jacket, amid the clutter in Henny April's room, and thought of Flotman's youngsters; Abdullah, the dressmaker's husband; Tommy; Isaac. And Frances. Don't let them come on Frances, not Frances, not dear, dear Frances. The window lightened and the morning dribbled in, and Beukes shivered as the thoughts passed like pain through his mind.

Henny April came in and said: 'Listen, *ou* Buke, we got to go. I want to be gone before people notice any passengers. It's getting light. How long we still got to wait? It's a long drive too, and I got a schedule, like.' Even the business of contraband had a timetable.

'A little longer,' Beukes said, looking up from his thoughts. 'Just a few more minutes.'

The morning ushered the first sunlight into the sky, but it was still shadowy in the yard. Then the old mongrel started barking and Henny April went out again. Beukes stood up and heard him commanding the dog to be quiet in the name of Jesus. Then he shouted back for Beukes and Beukes went to the door and out into the yard.

He said, 'God's truth,' for there, in the dissolving shadows, holding a paper carrier as if he had come from market, stood Isaac.

Isaac came towards him, smiling, saying: 'Hullo, old Buke. I'm glad to see you're awright.'

'Ike, you bogger,' Beukes said happily. 'You old – dammit, is it you?' He was pumping Isaac's hand up and down, chuckling

178

and enjoying the sight of the protuberant ears, the expression of mild surprise. But there was something new too, in the slightly bulging eyes.

'It's me awright,' Isaac said. Then added, 'By the way, I'm Paul now, hey.'

'Paul, yes,' Beukes said, slapping his shoulders. 'Paul. And I never knew you had volunteered.'

'They got hold of me,' Isaac smiled as they stood there in the lightening yard. 'The bloody SP almost got hold of me too. But I managed okay.'

'I heard about it,' Beukes said. 'Well, dammit, it is a great thing you are doing, Ike.'

Isaac's ears turned pink, and he said seriously, 'It's just that we can't let them get away with it all the time, Buke.'

'I know, I know,' Beukes murmured, looking into the other's eyes. 'I know.'

Henny April came up and said, 'Buke, we have got to go, pal. There's too many people around already, they might notice us.'

'*Ja*, I reckon so,' Beukes said. The other two men were waiting, carrying their bundles. Isaac went over and shook hands with them. The children were coming from the house now, rubbing sleep from their eyes, and trailing into the yard, staring at the men assembled there.

'Isaac,' Beukes said, 'you look after yourself, hey.'

'I'll do that, Buke,' Isaac nodded. 'I'll do that.' They went over towards the van. 'Listen, Buke,' he added, 'There's my ma and sister. If you could sort of let them know I'm awright?'

'I'll let them know, Ike.'

'And there's those two boys who was working with me. I got their addresses written down here. You get in touch with them, Buke, they're awright.'

'I won't forget.'

Maria had come to the door of the house, standing big, and Henny April went over to talk to her. He came back again, patting the heads of the children in the yard. It was quite light now, and the yard was revealing its shape; the piles of tyres, the spare parts, the washlines. In the street, people were starting to pass, heading for the bus-stops.

'Okay, Beukes, not to worry,' Henny April said.

Beukes smiled at him. 'I'm not worrying at all, chum.'

'Take care that arm, hey.'

They were at the van again and Beukes raised a hand, saluting the three young men who sat inside, on the padded seats which had been fitted to the floor. Henny April had loaded his suitcases.

Beukes shook hands with Peter and Michael and said, 'Remember, you stick to those names: Paul and Michael.' Then added, feeling warm, 'So long, soldiers.' He turned to Isaac and said again, 'So long, soldier, you too.'

Beukes saluted them once more and Henny April slammed the rear doors of the van and the last Beukes saw of them was Peter's straw boater and Isaac looking up to peer out through the rear window – the look of slight surprise and the prominent ears. Henny April climbed behind the wheel and shut the door. He looked out while the motor ground into life, the exhaust banged, and he backed the van slowly out of the yard.

Beukes walked by the van to the street. Henny April waved to his wife and said to Beukes, 'Well, I'll see these boggers get safe where they got to go.'

The sun was brightening the east now, clearing the roofs of the suburb and the new light broke the shadows into scattered shapes. Henny April waved again, and Beukes watched the old van turn into the street and then it was wheeling away between the soiled houses, the scanty garden-lots, leaving behind a mist of blue smoke.

Beukes stood by the side of the street in the early morning and thought, they have gone to war in the name of a suffering people. What the enemy himself has created, these will become battle-grounds, and what we see now is only the tip of an ice-berg of resentment against an ignoble regime, the tortured victims of hatred and humiliation. And those who persist in hatred and humiliation must prepare. Let them prepare hard and fast – they do not have long to wait.

He stood there until the van was out of sight and then turned back to where the children had gathered in the sunlit yard.

NELSON MANDELA
No Easy Walk to Freedom

A collection of the articles, speeches, letters and trials of the most important figure in the South African liberation struggle.

OLIVER TAMBO
Preparing for Power – Oliver Tambo Speaks

This selection of speeches, interviews and letters offers a unique insight into the ANC Chairman's views on the history of the freedom struggle within South Africa and, of even greater importance, his vision for the future.

DORIS LESSING
The Grass is Singing

The classic murder story of the Rhodesian farmer's wife and her houseboy.

NADINE GORDIMER
Some Monday for Sure

Nadine Gordimer has used these stories from her five collections to tell of the daily frustrations and contradictions of life in South African society.

THE AFRICAN AND CARIBBEAN WRITERS SERIES

The book you have been reading is part of Heinemann's long-established series of African and Caribbean fiction. Details of some of the other titles available are given below, but for a catalogue giving information on the whole Series write to: Heinemann International Literature and Textbooks, Halley Court, Jordan Hill, Oxford OX2 8EJ

NGŨGĨ WA THIONG'O
Matigari

This is a moral fable telling the story of a freedom fighter and his quest for Truth and Justice. The novel is set in the political dawn of post-independence Kenya.
'Clear, subtle, mischievous, passionate novel'. *Sunday Times*

Devil on the Cross

Written secretly in prison, on lavatory paper, while the author was detained without trial, this novel is a powerful critique of modern Kenya.

A Grain of Wheat

'With Mr Ngũgĩ, history is living tissue. He writes with poise from deep reserves, and the book adds cubits to his already considerable stature.' *The Guardian*

Petals of Blood

A compelling novel about the tragedy of corrupting power, set in post-independence Kenya.
'. . . Ngũgĩ writes with passion about every form, shape and colour which power can take'. *Sunday Times*

Weep Not, Child

This powerful, moving story about the effects of the Mau Mau war on the lives of ordinary men and women in Kenya is one of the best-known of Ngũgĩ's works. 'This story is a skilful work of art'. *Times Literary Supplement*

The River Between

'A sensitive novel about the Gikuyu in the melting pot that sometimes touches the grandeur of tap-root simplicity'. *The Guardian*

CHINUA ACHEBE
Things Fall Apart

This, the first title in the African Writers Series, describes how a man in the Igbo tribe of South Africa became exiled from the tribe and returned only to be forced to commit suicide to escape the results of his rash courage against the white man.

STEVE BIKO
I Write What I Like

'An impressive tribute to the depth and range of his thought, covering such diverse issues as the basic philosophy of black consciousness, Bantustans, African culture, the institutional church, and Western involvement in apartheid.' *The Catholic Herald*